TROPIC OF PASSION

&

AMAZON GOLD FEVER

Two Tales of Jungle Adventure

by

CHARLES NUETZEL

WRITING AS "JOHN DAVIDSON"

The Borgo Press
An Imprint of Wildside Press

MMVII

CONTENTS

BOOK TWO: AMAZON GOLD FEVER

ABOUT THE AUTHOR

Charles Nuetzel was born in San Francisco in 1934, and writes:

"As long as I can remember I wanted to be a writer. It was a dream I never thought would materialize. But with the help of Forrest J Ackerman, who became my agent, I managed to finally make it into print.

"I was lucky enough not only in selling my work to publishers but also ending up packaging books for some of them, and finally becoming a 'publisher' much like those who had bought my first novels. From there it as a simple leap to editing not only a sci-fi anthology, but a line of sci-fi books for Powell Sci-Fi back in the 1960s. Throughout these active professional years I had the chance to design some covers and do graphic cover layouts for pocket books & magazines."

Much of his work in covers and graphics are a result of having had a father who was a professional commercial artist, and who did a number of covers for sci-fi magazines in the 1950s and later for pocket books—even for some of Mr. Nuetzel's books.

In retirement he has become involved in swing dancing, a long time lover of Big Band jazz. But more interestingly world travels have taken him (and his wife Brigitte) across the world, to Hawaii, Caribbean, Mexico, Kenya, Egypt, Peru, having a lifelong interest in ancient civilizations. His website is full of thousands of pictures taken during these trips.

INTRODUCTION

I don't mind admitting that *Tropic of Passion* was just a bit shorter than I expected, and so you, the reader, are offered not only this novel, but a nice little adventure short as a bonus: *Amazon Gold Fever*.

The major story in this adventure duo was one of my early novels, which has been somewhat altered here to make it "even better" than before! Actually, in re-reading the book after so many years I had a different take on the subject and offered up some basic improvements, but not too many as to change the fun of it all.

Here we have a man down on his luck that gets a chance to improve his life when a woman named Ruby offers him an adventure and riches beyond his wildest dreams. (That sounds just about right! Even intrigues me!)

As it says on the cover: *They came for ancient treasure only to discover death, destruction and love...*

Well, okay, we've all been there time and again, and continue to return to enjoy the adventure and the excitement and the intrigue!

So, I'm an all-day sucker for those ancient relics and ruined remains of lost civilizations. There's a kind of romantic ecstasy to be discovered in such places. The imagination just runs wild. What kind of people lived back there, what were their passions all about, what drove them to do what they did? Why did they insist on offering young virgins to their lusty, passion-hungry gods of old?

Such questions can drive the mind to the very edge of madness!

Well, this ain't no Time Travel sci-fi flick or novel. So such questions are left unanswered. This is just your basic adventure, a walk down a colorful jungle passageway into the arms of...

Stop! You don't want me to give it all away right here and now, do ya all?

But I loved these make-believe worlds in my youth and still enjoy revisiting them from time to time. It is back to yesteryear when the wonderful worlds of Edgar Rice Burroughs flamed in blood to hot fire and raced young minds into adventures beyond the mundane boredom of every day life.

Okay. Life can be sweet. Lovely. Rich and passionate. Today's world offers up the computer and the Internet and cable television and so many other wonderful electronic toys that sometimes it is simply difficult to keep up! So in such moments we can, if we so desire, step backwards make a graceful turn into the adventure zone!

And to add to the fun & games, I've inserted "Amazon Gold Fever," which almost seems too real to believe! Or rather it is difficult *not* to believe it actually happened to that poor fella who, for all I know, is still down there in South America seeking.

No! I won't say more! Let his story reveal his nightmares for all to enjoy!

BOOK ONE

Tropic of Passion

CHAPTER ONE

Dan Shon woke up with a dry taste in his mouth. For a moment he thought he was still in the city of the dead. But he was getting used to that. For weeks now he had been having nightmares. But it was getting better. He knew that with time they would go away.

He glanced at the woman in bed with him, experiencing all the emotions that had flooded into being on that distant island so short a time before. It was strange how things had happened. In such a short time his life had changed dramatically.

Just a little over two months before...

* * * * * * *

He had been standing on the porch of his small beach cottage, looking out at the ocean, when her voice broke into his thoughts.

"Hi, Dan!" the woman's soft, low voice broke into his thoughts.

For a moment he couldn't focus, captured only by the bright, low quality of her greeting.

Then he saw the woman and remembered.

Ruby West.

She was dressed in a flaring skirt and blouse tied

around her waist, just under the full curve of her breasts, and it was open at the top. The effect was a sensational showing of the rounded shape of her bust-line. Her face had an inner flush to it, but her whole attitude was slightly reserved.

They'd met only a couple of weeks ago. A few nights ago they had almost come to his place.

Her voice was soft, bright and so damned seductive when she spoke.

"I just didn't have anything to do tonight—and hoped you were...well, were free for the evening. You said to drop in any time. You know how it gets—sometimes?" she had offered by way of explanation. It was an excuse, but not the reason. But he didn't care about reasons; they didn't matter. That she was there was all that mattered. He'd wanted to get intimate with her at first sight.

"And, anyway, I needed to see you, Dan." Ruby plunked down into a bamboo chair on the front porch. "Really. We need to talk."

She sounded all business.

His eyes sweep over her body. Then he looked at her lovely face. Those lips were soft looking and so damned kissable. "What about?"

"Well, to be truthful, Dan...well...nothing to do with the obvious. Oh, that, too, I suppose." She grinned up at him, eyes quite serious. "I really like you. We both have...the hots for one another. I know that."

"Well, that's blunt." He grinned wolfishly at her.

"Sometimes it seems right. Being blunt. Clears the air, you know." She was gazing directly into his eyes and there was a shimmering seductiveness showing, but clouded over by something else far more serious. "Do you mind?"

"Mind what?" All he could think of was getting her body into his arms and ravishing it. And the implication of her being there, and her verbal gambit, certainly suggested that was exactly what would happen.

"Mind my being here." She studied him very seriously.

"Hell no!" he exploded. "I've been wanting to get you here for days."

"Really, now?" She sounded pleased. "Why didn't you push it?"

"I thought we did, the other night."

"Yes. It was annoying things didn't work out. All that confusion. Friends can be a pain."

"Yes," he remembered. A couple of people he knew had joined them and things just drifted away from escaping to his place. Conversations had lasted into the very late morning hours and by the time it had ended it was too late.

"Well, here I am," she stated. "But...we need to...talk about something important...first."

She fell silent for a moment, seemingly uncertain.

He offered: "How about a drink?"

After the drinks had been served and Ruby had finished off half of hers, she looked across at where he was standing. For a moment Ruby's mouth opened to say something and then she stopped. Then she looked up at Dan once more and said: "We've known each other for only a short time. But I feel that I—that I know you enough...I feel we are friends..."

11

Ruby's voice faded out then, but she continued to gaze up at him, evenly. Then her face flushed pink for a moment and she continued: "What I'm trying to say is that...could I ask you a favor?"

That one surprised Dan. He hardly knew what to say to it—how to react.

Then nervously she added: "I was going to...let things...develop first before asking. Let nature take its course, so to speak. But that wouldn't be very nice, I suppose. Business before pleasure."

"What did you have in mind?" Dan asked carefully, his business sense now on complete alert.

"Well..." she smiled, almost seductive, "beyond the obvious...I mean, you and me, and all we've been...dishing out at one another..."

"Well? Go on." Dan was both intrigued and annoyed. All he could think of was getting her in his arms.

"It's about—about your boat."

"The Sea Witch?"

"Yes." Ruby took another swallow of her drink and then continued: "There's an island some two or three hundred miles northwest of here that I have to get to—"

"So?"

"So I was wondering if—if you'd take me there?"

"Well, that's the business I'm in," Dan pointed out guardedly. He made an effort not to have put too much force on the word "business" but that was the message he wanted to put across. It was a business, not charity.

"I have to get there! There'll be money in it, once we arrive, but—but I don't have any right

12

now."

That did it. The flirtation was very possibly a cover to get his attention—and had nothing to do with interest in him as a man!

Bitterly he downed the rest of his drink and then looked away from Ruby. Social was one thing. Business another.

He felt both a deep sense of hurt and annoyance, and anger at himself for feeling that way. And he felt a sense of disappointment with the woman. He had almost thought she was in some way special. Why should that be? It didn't make sense. They'd flirted, toyed around with the idea of getting intimate, but nothing more.

When he looked in her direction again she was standing, starting to slip out of her blue skirt.

"What the hell?" was Dan's first reaction. He saw too clearly what Ruby was about to do. "That's not going to do you any good!"

Ruby simply smiled up at him, slowly untying her blouse. As the cloth was pulled aside, the fullness of her breasts surged outward, naked and brimming over with silky, supple looking flesh. Their pink centers seemed to call to him with an honest eagerness. There was no faking that. Then slowly Ruby slipped her fingers under the elastic of her panties and urged them downward until she stood completely nude before him.

She said nothing, but merely stood there, quite confident in her sexuality and the effect she had on a man—on him.

All Dan could do was to stand there, gaping at her. Burning desire shortened his breath. It wasn't possible to look at her without being totally overwhelmed.

Ruby glided slowly toward the doorway leading to Dan's one small bedroom. She smiled and then stepped over the threshold. She was totally confident that he would follow her.

Like a wooden zombie Dan stepped into the bedroom, quickly stripping. His eyes caressed over Ruby's naked form which now lying on the bed.

Throwing his clothes aside, Dan moved down next to her.

She murmured: "I've wanted this...since we met."

He said nothing, but covered her lips with hot, hungry kisses. She leaned up into him, her mouth open, tongue eagerly seeking his. Their bodies fairly raged against one another. She was a wild storm of sheer, passionate electricity.

The world momentarily had clouded around Dan and become blackness.

Then, next thing he knew, he was alone in bed. Awareness that Ruby wasn't next to him moved Dan instantly from the bed. He quickly dressed, wondering what had happened to her.

The bloody woman had seduced him royally and then vanished!

CHAPTER TWO

At mid-morning Ruby appeared carrying a small leather handbag. He had been anxiously awaiting her arrival.

"Well, hi!" she greeted, moving close to Dan and kissing him lightly on the cheek.

Dan looked at her, silently questioning. Wondering how she'd managed to bewitch him so quickly. It was pure, raw sex, he realized that.

The rest, he just didn't know. She was a total mystery. Warning bells continued to ring in the back of his brain.

Yet he couldn't help himself.

She smiled: "Ready to take me off into the sunset? When the sun sets, that is."

After brushing back his blond hair, he took a step back, away from her. "Yes. Sure. But...you really have me spinning."

"I hope in a nice way."

"Crazy way."

"Crazy?" she thought that over then asked: "Why crazy?"

"Well, you've a puzzle."

"Hardly. Straight forward. I really don't like playing games," she told him, quite seriously.

"I mean...well...I just don't...get you."

Ruby laughed brightly; it was a bubbling sound floating on the warm morning air. "What is there to get?"

Plenty, he thought, both pleased and puzzled.

He said: "Well…last night…"

"Yes. It was wonderful. Wasn't it?"

"And you didn't tell me very much."

"Yes, I know," she offered, winking playfully. "You were terribly sweet about it."

"Sweet?"

She stepped close, giving him a soft kiss. "Yes. Very sweet. And more, I might add." She hefted the small bag in her right hand. "Where can I drop this?"

He shrugged. She placed it on the floor near the door to his small beach shack. Turned and faced him. "Well, I wonder what we can do for the rest of the day."

Christ, he thought, *plenty*.

"I don't…get you."

"Yes you do." She laughed at that. "Well, you did and can…that is."

"You know what I mean. How can I put it nicely?" He sighed, then said, rather bluntly: "You offer certain favors for taking you…"

Ruby's frown cut him short. "I didn't think you'd take it that way."

"How else *could* I take it?" Dan exploded in surprise.

"Cheer up. I simply asked you to take me away on your boat…" Ruby's lips spread into a sensual smile and then she patted Dan on the cheek. "And I said I'd pay you. Later. What's so strange about that?"

16

"Usually I get an advance."

"Wasn't last night...a *nice* advance?" she offered in a light, teasing voice.

"Don't cheapen it like that! I'm talking about hard...."

She laughed at that, cutting his words off. "You offered that...if I remember right."

"Oh, come on," he retorted, finding it difficult to keep his eyes off her lush body. "Cash is what I'm talking about."

"Is that really all you're interested in?" She came closer, standing a couple of feet away, just within reach.

She, again, just smiled up into his eyes, very warmly, yet a bit mysteriously, holding back just a little.

"You haven't changed your mind—?" Ruby frowned for a moment, and then her full but delicate features relaxed to become expressionless.

"No. Just don't like being kept in the dark."

And feeling like a class-A fool, he silently added to himself.

"I guess...I shouldn't have tried to bribe you that way."

"Well...better than no bribe, I suppose," he admitted.

Ruby frowned, said: "I can't tell you much right now. You'll have to trust me. We leave tonight. After dark. In secret."

Dan wanted to shout out questions. He wanted to express his doubts, but instead he just nodded. "Okay."

"I guess you think this is all very strange," Ruby said. "But believe me, it *is* important. You'll find out why it is so important—later. I promise."

"W*hat's the mystery?"*

Ruby sighed: "Maybe I *should* tell you something. That is ... enough so that you'll maybe—well, understand a little." She broke off, staring deep into his eyes. "The most I can tell you right now is that I'm going out to meet my brother. He's been searching for...for something let's say—of great importance—or value. But only...well, Dan, I can't, just can't tell you any more. Except that the trip might not end there. But by then...you'll know more...and...well, it'll seem different."

Ruby smiled. "Please, Dan, let's not talk about it any more." She slid her arms around his neck and he felt the light pressure of her hips surge up against his. "We have the rest of the day..."

Suddenly Ruby was straining boldly against Dan. Her breasts crushed hard to his chest and he could feel the firm, suggestive circling of her hips as they surged forward.

The sweetness of her kiss was filled with all the savage passion and normal female lust for a man. All at once Dan didn't care any more about questions. His body cried out for the soothing fire that Ruby could bathe over it, which would start the volcanic boil inside his groin.

And even as he lifted her into his arms and carried her to the bedroom, Dan knew she wanted to end the questions, and had done it in the most effective way possible—with her body. Just like the night before when she had appeared at his small beach cottage.

* * * * * *

Two hundred miles away on a large island, covered by tropical palms and ferns, in a hotel room, old and shabby, a nervous young man sat at a small table, looking at a bulky old manuscript, his eyes brightly glassed over. There was a bottle of rum sitting within easy reach of his thin, wiry fingers. He'd read the manuscript many times before, yet the fascination of its tale still fired his imagination.

He paused for a moment to reach for the bottle of rum, taking a long drag from the neck of it. "Ruby, oh, sister Ruby—wait till you see this!" he shouted out loud, anxiously returning his gaze to the manuscript.

The paper was dirty and old, but the printing was still sharp and readable.

He read half to himself and half aloud:

> ...I have always felt there was some honest truth to the theory of a lost continent in the Pacific Ocean. Maybe it was a dream—maybe based on some intuition. But that doesn't really matter.
>
> And even if what I've found here doesn't prove or disprove the theory of a Continent of Mu, that doesn't matter, either. For in reality, what I've found is worth a fortune—boundless treasures of an age that disappeared long before the known history of man. Before Egypt. Maybe even before the cave man. Maybe there was more to that book on Haldolen than mere fiction. I always wondered and dreamed of such

a place. I only saw the original manuscript once, but considered it more fiction than fact. Yet that was supposed to
have existed something like 30,000
BC! A huge, ancient, civilization which
had spread its colonies out beyond its
own land mass, supposedly within the
Pacific Ocean, now submerged and
gone forever. Well, no matter. Maybe
aliens from outer space for all we
know. Fiction is wild with inviting
theories. Science bows only to hard
fact—even when inspired by fantasy
and myth and legend. All are just an
endless puzzle that drives all of us to
seek the unknown, discovering new
clues into the past.

For who knows what existed in all
the infinity of time, before man came
into being on this little speck of clay
we call Earth? But of what importance
is this? The time and place may some
day be recorded.

Quickly he turned the pages toward the back of the
manuscript, picking up the portion from which he
wished to continue:

...Now I know that the location and the
existence of this island and its ancient
treasure must forever be kept locked in
time—a secret. What I have discovered
here is far too unsettling for me to ac-
cept...

He put down the papers and looked across at the far wall, his almost boyish features taking on a twisted frown. Slowly the frown changed to a thin, crooked laugh.

"Dear, dear little foolish uncle! Mad, insane scientist! But you won't be getting in our way any more. You'll never worry about what *we* uncover—and what we 'let loose'... what 'strange powers'!" Standing up, the man laughed; the sound bounced from wall to wall like a scream from a madhouse. "Finally, at last, it's all gonna be ours!"

He wanted to celebrate. It was only a matter of a few hours, now. Ever since he'd radioed Ruby to come and meet him here, he'd been in a state of drunken excitement. After all the years of waiting, they were really ready to move—to rediscover what their mad uncle had been afraid to expose to the modern world. The crazy old man.

A bitter laugh broke from his weak lips as he moved across the room, staggering slightly. He got as far as the door before he slowly slid down to the floor, unconscious.

* * * * * * *

The hours with Ruby had been deliciously passionate, and exhausting. Late in the afternoon he took her to the *Sea Witch,* only to discover that his one and only crew member, wasn't on board. So he left Ruby there, to settle in, and went out to get his first mate.

Dan found Billy Turk at the local watering hole not far from where the Sea Witch was docked. He hurriedly got him out of the place before Billy had a chance to object.

"I'm going to need you, Billy!" Dan told the heavy, barrel-chested man.

"Not again! Thought we'd be stayin' round for a spell, matie. What's the rushin'?"

"Gather your gear and be on deck within an hour!" Dan ordered his first and only mate.

"Okay—okay! And just when I was up to makin' a point with a lady!" Billy Turk growled. "Anythin' you say, matie!"

CHAPTER THREE

The two shadows moved like black things from another world, onto the small schooner. The night air was beginning to blow up speed, and the darkness of the sky threatened an ugly whisper of a storm. Low, dangerous clouds hid the moon. Slowly the sailing vessel started out to sea, like a tiny splinter of wood facing the unknown, powerful breaths of the sea gods.

Time passed and the ocean chopped at the sides of the little *Sea Witch,* whose tiny but powerful motor pushed it forward across the black waters. The sky darkened and a distant rumble shattered the world, as a flashing explosion of electricity crackled at the horizon.

There was one light showing from the cabin porthole that sliced the darkness surrounding the tiny craft with its narrow, dim beam. Inside, two people were sitting at a small, crude table. There was a bottle between them.

Ruby's loud laugh cut into the air of the small room. She leaned forward, toward Dan, smiling, a savage light in her eyes. "When will you stop worrying? I told you that everything is all right! You'll just have to trust me!"

After a moment, Ruby sighed and said in a more

serious manner, "I'll give you this much, if you promise to stop asking questions."

Dan nodded, grimly.

"I got the radiogram from my brother yesterday.

"That's why I suddenly asked you for this little *favor*. I'll not fool you or lie—I came to this island for the purpose of receiving a message and meeting my brother.

"Now that we're on our way...well...I'll tell you: my uncle was a hobby archaeologist. Years ago he found *something* here in the South Pacific—but he kept it secret. He died recently—we got hold of his papers, being his only living relatives.

"My brother has those papers, and we'll be going to the island they tell about. If you want to go with us...but that will be up to you, I suppose.

"First, I have to get to my brother. That's all I can tell you, and the only reason I go that far, now, is that we're out in the middle of nowhere, and there isn't any chance of anybody else hearing about it! Plus, I don't know much beyond that."

"That's a bit fantastic," Dan noted, a bit grimly.

"Not anywhere as...well you'll find out. Believe me, it'll blow your mind!" Ruby laughed loudly again and leaned back, her breasts pushed forward by the action, baring a valley view to Dan's gaze. "And there will be a lot more in it for you...I promise!"

"Okay—so I'll believe the story," Dan said tiredly. He wasn't sure if he did or not. There were a lot of loopholes in it; but there wasn't anything he could do about it right then.

He would wait.

Listen.

And when the time presented itself, he would decide.

"But I'm worried about this storm coming up," Dan commented, half standing. His face hardened, the muscles tightening.

"Oh, don't worry about that! You've got a mate up there to handle things!" Ruby pointed out, leaning forward again, looking hauntingly into Dan's eyes.

The expression on her face was as readable as a book: she wanted him to stay...

Angrily Dan sat, reaching for the bottle of rum and taking a large swallow from it. Blast women, he thought bitterly, gulping more rum before laying it down on the table between the two of them.

He was an all-day sucker for a beautiful body!

That dream still bothered him, too. Not that he felt it meant anything; but rather because it was the first time he'd ever really experienced such a terrible nightmare.

All his life, Dan had been willing to let things fall where they might, not caring about anything—not even about his own life. Nothing had mattered to him for years—not since his wife had died a decade ago.

Dan tensed visibly at the thought of his wife. He'd managed to keep her out of his mind for years. Why should she return now? What had caused him to think of Gloria? Then all of a sudden he realized the truth.

He peered at Ruby and felt a shock run through his body. He could almost see Gloria's face in Ruby's. His wife hadn't been quite as attractive and not really so olive-skinned, but there was enough sameness about the two women to be almost startling.

They both had delicate but sensual features. Ruby's eyes were a little larger and a little darker, and her lips more full and cushiony, yet the general tone was the same.

"What's wrong, Dan?" Ruby asked, leaning closer. "What's wrong?"

"Oh, nothing!" Dan said, standing up. "It's just that need to be alone for a while. Nothing personal, just..."

"When will you come back...soon?"

Dan nodded.

"I'll be ready."

Dan walked out of the main cabin and onto the deck, stepping over to Billy Turk, who was standing by the wheel. "How are things?"

Billy nodded, grinning. "How're things, matie?"

For a moment Dan only looked at his first mate, and then simply smiled and stepped around the other man. He wanted to think a little. The sudden realization of why Ruby had attracted him so much had been unsettling. The idea of making love to her seemed abruptly strange—it was like sleeping with his dead wife.

Yet that was silly.

Gloria had been a wonderful woman and a good wife, and they had lived normal and sane lives. He had met her in high school and when they were nineteen they got married. It had lasted until Gloria had died suddenly in childbirth. And then Dan had simply tried to blot out his life with her by coming to the islands to live. Escaping all that he had been by running to something that was so alien and different that it was impossible to have memory symbols of places where he had been with Gloria. In some ways it had been possible to forget her and the life they had shared.

Now she had come out of the past, in the form of Ruby West, to haunt him. It was silly to feel that way, but...

Actually, Dan reasoned, maybe it would be better to go back and enjoy himself with Ruby. Gloria was long gone—and Ruby was alive.

He turned and said to Billy, "You'll be okay?"

"Through the worst storm!" the man nodded.

Dan moved toward the cabin, as if pulled by a power beyond his control.

As he stepped into the cabin, closing the door behind him and bolting it, he didn't at first see Ruby.

Then he noticed a bare leg showing over the edge of the lower bunk. Maybe that really *was* the answer. Escape in Ruby. Ruby's body was waiting there for Dan to take, and he couldn't resist. As if controlled by an outside force, Dan undressed and moved to the bunk. A moment later he was in her arms, feeling the silkiness of her body surge up against his.

Her lips, anxious, warm, moist and open, clung to his; her tongue whipped out, searching and seeking with a thrusting rhythm that pulled him into such a fury of passion and lust that he couldn't think about anything but the consummation of that desire.

* * * * * * *

The storm swelled up around the schooner,

27

whipping it back and forth across the tortured ocean. The skies moaned like some living thing.

Billy Turk stayed at the wheel, holding the boat on the fine side of survival, a triumphant smile spreading across his thick, ruddy features.

The storm finally passed with the night. But Billy didn't hear from Dan Shon and he didn't worry. He only wondered what had bewitched his boss. But it wasn't for him to question. He was paid for a job and that was the end of it. Where Dan took him, he would go, for he owed his life to Dan.

The hours went by, Billy in control of the schooner and Dan and Ruby hidden away in their cabin, shelled in away from the world of reality. Finally their destination slowly rose on the far horizon. The island drifted toward them from the edge of the world.

When there was less than an hour to go, Dan stepped out onto the deck, Ruby at his side. There was a look of utter helplessness in his eyes and something else that Billy couldn't quite fathom.

Then the island took complete possession of the horizon, and finally the small boat slipped into the harbor and docked at the small wooden pier.

CHAPTER FOUR

Carl West sat looking at the shadowy face sitting across the booth from him. There was a nasty grind making his insides want to shoot up over the table. For a moment he dropped his eyes down to the bottle of rum in front of him, his hand reaching out instinctively for it.

If Ruby found out the mess he was in, he thought, nervously pulling the bottle to his lips and taking several swallows from it. But what bothered him most was the fact that Gordon had found him. Carl had been sure that he was safe from the gambling syndicate.

He was sure they wouldn't have been able to find him here. That had been one of the reasons he had made sure that things were arranged so that his uncle's manuscript would get into his hands at this time, so that he could get the treasure, and from that money pay off the hundreds of thousands he owed.

The man opposite him had a hard darkness to his features, and a crooked short scar mounting his face on the right cheek.

"I don't know," Carl finally said in a slow drawl. "It's not the money, you know. We'll have plenty of that—just give me a couple of more months,"

"And have you slip out of civilized existence? That's big money you owe. If we let you get away with it...how could we ever be sure somebody might hear and...you can see how it is?"

"But I'll have the money—believe me! There's a deal coming...I'll pay you with interest!"

"Look, Mr. West," the other snapped firmly, in a rasping bass voice. "Either—or. You pay up or you'll find yourself dead! I was sent to get the money or drop your body in the blue Pacific." Desperately the younger man looked up at the scarred man. "My sister is coming here—she should be arriving tonight or tomorrow. I can't touch any money. We need it to make a big killing."

"What?" The man's hard eyes took on the glint of knowing interest.

"I can't tell you about that!"

There was a moment of silence, and then finally the scar-faced man asked in a low whisper: "Does it have anything to do with *The Virgin Venus?*"

Carl tensed in surprise. His face went white and then shaded red. Nervously he reached for the bottle but the other's hand jumped faster, taking the rum out of reach.

"I know about it. All about it. That's why. Let's say that's why I'm willing to do business with you."

"But how?"

"Never you mind about that. We have our ways."

"But..."

"No but! Pay up the money or you cut me in!"

"I *can't* do that!" Carl cried in terrified agony. "It's *impossible!*"

The bigger man reached out a huge, thick hand,

clasping his heavy fingers on the front of Carl's shirt. "Now you listen to me, little boy! And get it straight. I get cut in or you disappear. *Right this night!* You get me?"

Carl gulped and then stammered, "I'll have to talk to Ruby."

"You talk good, or you're *dead!*" The man's hand relaxed, and then he stood. "You just remember that. We'll see you tomorrow. Got me?" Then without another word he moved from the tavern, leaving Carl alone with his agonized thoughts.

The young man gripped the bottle of rum, put the neck up to his lips and started gulping. Fifteen minutes later he got up and staggered out of the bar and onto the small, narrow dirt street, moving in the direction of his hotel room.

The air was hot and moist, the night dark. He moved in a half run and finally staggered into the small hotel where he was staying. Walking into the lobby, Carl was called over by the desk clerk.

"There's a woman waiting for you."

"Ruby West?"

"I don't know, she didn't leave her name. Just said you were her brother. I let her into your room."

Carl moved across the lobby, toward the stairway leading to the top, second floor. A few moments later he opened the door to his room.

Ruby was standing there, nervously stamping out a cigarette. She didn't smile, just glared at him, anger showing on her pretty features.

* * * * * * *

Dan Shon stood on the deck of the boat, nervously smoking a cigarette and looking out toward the shore. It had been three hours since Ruby West had left the boat, going to shore, demanding that he stay there and wait for her.

Dan was just about to turn and walk into the cabin, when he saw a small dinghy coming toward him. For a moment he gazed in that direction, and saw there were two people in the boat. One was a woman. In a few moments he recognized her dark hair, and then as the small dinghy came closer, he made out her delicate features.

A few moments later Dan was helping Ruby up onto the deck, and then a small-built young man followed her aboard. Ruby's first words were a command: "Get the hell out of here, and fast!"

"What the—" Dan started to say, stepping back in his shock at the sharp expression of nervous fear twisting Ruby's pretty features.

"Hurry, there's no time!" she ordered, in a tight, shaking voice. "I'll tell you everything when we're out to sea."

Twenty minutes later they were putting as much distance as possible between themselves and the island. Billy Turk was at the wheel and Dan, Ruby and Carl West were in the cabin.

Ruby was talking. "There's this island, where at one time we believe there was some kind of vast civilization...well, you've heard the lost continent theory. We believe that it...we think that Uncle Frank found a segment of what was known by some as Mu. A huge continent, once thriving in the Pacific and which sank.

"The remains that our uncle found contain a vast treasure. It took him years to find it. All we need now is a boat like yours. And secrecy. That, above all else.

"But some crooks have discovered what Carl is after—and they wanted to be cut in. That's why we had to get out of there and fast!"

"You mean we're going to the ruins of...a lost...civilization?" Dan said in an awed voice. "You gotta be kidding."

"I'm deadly serious, Dan. That's exactly what we are going to do!"

CHAPTER FIVE

Jim Gordon stared at the blonde woman and sighed, trying to focus through the dimness of the whiskey he had been drinking. He found his eyes centered on the large nipples of her breasts, contemplating them in the most sensual way.

Anna Torrie was one hell of a hot bitch in heat.

"Anna. You're a real thriller!" he hissed, gulping some more liquor from the bottle.

"You've been staring at me for almost an hour, drinking and boozing, but ain't you goin' to do something for me?" she demanded in a coarse, rasping voice. "You make me strip and then you just stare." She moved on the bed, giving him a full view of her naked body.

"You hot bitch!" he gasped, his eyes following the wide, large curves of her breasts and hips. "You're one loving, whoring bitch! Love that about you!"

"Then do something about it, honey. I'm getting so horny!"

For a moment he almost stood up from the small chair he was sitting in, then he relaxed and took another swallow of his drink. It was good making her beg for it. Then he laughed. "That Carl West. We got him bugged but good!"

"I suppose!" Anna sighed, sat up, gazing evenly at the man.

"Yeah, he became a trembling chicken shit! Oh, they're gonna crush my balls! Oh, lordy, lordy, save me from the evil mod-monsters!" He laughed loud and hard. "He almost pissed in his pants!"

The woman's eyes grew more intense as she considered him. A deeply interested expression showed on her face. "And *The Virgin Venus?* Tell me more about that!"

"Oh, he'll cough up the information, and then we'll be rich for life!"

Anna shrugged, now beginning to relax a little, realizing the game he was playing. It was a game she wouldn't play into. She smiled and picked up a bottle from the floor next to the bed. She gulped on the rum. "Tell me again. Tell me how you found out about the Venus Idol!"

"That's simple!" Gordon explained eager to re-hash the tale once more. "Me and a man named Mark Jennings were in the pen together. He tells me everything about himself. And about his father. His father was the assistant to a Dr. West many years ago, when the good doctor went on this scientific expedition or something in the islands.

"I learned about it just a little too late. The old man—this West cat—was dead. Well, I find out that he left the whole bit to his brother's children who were hot for it. So I arrange for the Carl guy to get into some games—you know, he likes to play the cards a little—and I fix it up so that he doesn't win—and he's had it. Scared to death that I'm with the Syndicate, and things like that. You know all the rest."

"Tell me about the Venus Idol!" Anna pressed him.

"*The Venus Idol*!" Gordon's eyes glazed over even more. "This Mark Tennings said it was in a temple or something—I don't know. On the island. Inlaid with all kinds of jewels. All we gotta do is to take a little knife and pull out all the jewels, and we'll have enough to keep us forever!"

"There's got to be a catch!"

"Catch? A curse, so this Dr. West said. That's why he wouldn't touch anything. Said there's a curse on the temple and everything in it."

"How'd he know?"

"Some way of reading what was on the temple walls. I don't know." Suddenly Gordon was irritated. He gazed at the woman and all at once found himself not wanting to talk any more. All he wanted to do was walk over to her and enjoy that lavish body.

"To hell with it all!" he cried, standing up and staggering over to the bed. "Let's not talk any more!"

Anna smiled up at him and then opened her arms as he slid down to her. She'd won her prize without begging. They locked drunkenly together, their lips meeting, parted and moist. After a while they weren't just kissing. Then he entered her, almost savagely and she screamed out in shear ecstasy as the very hardness of him thrashed at her again and again so voluptuously big that she almost felt she would die in the very pleasure of it all. He then took his time and she rode him for a very long time. Then later the rhythm of their bodies on the bed caused a nerve-racking rasp that neither of them noticed. Nothing existed other than the union of their bodies in their final ecstatic climax that left nothing beyond exhausted sleep.

It was late in the morning before Gordon stirred, and then he lay still for a long time afterwards. An hour later he was sliding out of bed and began to get dressed.

His head was hammering, but he hardly noticed. Walking from the room, he started down the hall just as Anna slipped out of bed and went into the shower.

It was late in the afternoon when Gordon returned to the hotel room, his face distorted in rage and his hands shaking.

"That goddamned bastard took off!" he screamed, slamming the door and rushing over to where Anna was sitting reading a movie magazine. "That damned son-of-a-bitch...he's gone!"

For a long moment Anna stared up at him, not saying anything, then she slowly stood and said:

"But don't you know where the island is? I thought you knew where the island was?"

"You little whore! Of course I know. But I don't know where the temple is—or how to get into it. We need the manuscript for that. If it weren't for that, we'd have gone a long time ago and cleaned up!"

It was several seconds before either of them spoke and then Gordon snapped: "Get packed and dressed—we're leaving! We'll follow them. Then on the island we can take care of them—get the papers and then the jewels.

"Nothin' matters but that—" Gordon broke off and glared at Anna. "Well, get up—hurry!" he screamed, his face distorting in rage. "Hurry, you bitch!"

Anna's face reddened as he yelled at her, but she slowly stood.

"I'll have to hire a couple of men and then a boat and then—then we'll be after those damned bastards!" Gordon yelled, rushing out of the room. "I'll be back later—I'll expect you then! You be ready to leave. Understand?"

Anna only nodded as she pulled out the clothing from the dresser and began to pack it in a suitcase. The moment the door slammed after Gordon, she stepped over to the nightstand next to the bed and picked up the bottle of rum sitting there.

Maybe she was a fool to hang around that rat Jim Gordon, she thought angrily, gulping on the bottle. *He wasn't the only male to enjoy. But maybe he would turn up with the fortune he had been promising her for the last couple of years. Maybe then it would all be worth it. Maybe...*

She sighed, tiredly, wearily, and then began packing again.

CHAPTER SIX

Dan Shon stood out on the deck, looking at the morning sun. His throat felt like a dry desert. The throb of his head was happily hammering away, sending pains through his skull. But he didn't really notice. The salt sea air was a good-tasting breakfast to his body; coupled with the rising sun, it was a stimulating shot in his guts. Strangely, regardless of everything, he felt good.

After she had arrived with her brother and they had set sail, she had disappeared in her cabin with Carl and he hadn't seen her since. The relaxation of an evening without sex had done him good.

A man had to be alone, once in a while, he thought, looking at the red and orange horizon. *It did a man good!*

He'd been a sucker for a beautiful broad for so many years that he couldn't remember when his first woman had caught him in her lovely web. He'd almost been weaned on sexy women. His much-too-short marriage with Gloria had been his only hitch with one woman for a period longer than six months.

Dan shrugged off the thought of his dead wife. She was one woman he didn't like to think about any more. It brought too much pain to him, and he didn't want to live in a world of the past. There was only the future and the present.

He had read once that a person should use the present as best he could, trying to build for the future. He thought it was Emerson who had said: *"The past is for us, but the sole terms on which it can become ours are its subordination to the present."* So he had tried to forget the past pains and the past glories, and attempt to escape into the present in the South Seas.

Maybe that had been running; and maybe it had been the wrong use of the idea Emerson had been trying to express, but it had been his way of facing the future after his wife had died

Don't fall in love with a woman! That was his motto now. He'd managed to keep to it, too.

Dan turned and moved to the stairway leading to the cabins. He needed a little breakfast. Rum.

He was just stepping into his cabin when the door opposite his opened and Carl West walked out. For a moment the two men looked at each other without saying anything. And then Carl smiled and extending his hand: "I'm sorry I wasn't in much condition last night to talk to you—but something happened on the island that scared us...and I was a little on the drunk side, I guess."

There was a boyish innocence to his friendliness, and Dan couldn't help but like the man a little. "That's all right. I worked up quite a drunk myself last night—hope I didn't bother you..."

"Not a sound—not as far as I know."

Dan studied the man's face, taking in his thin, almost weak figure and then nodded.

"Come on in, then, maybe we can get to know

each other a little," Dan offered, stepping aside and motioning Carl into his cabin.

"Tell me, Carl, a little more about this little adventure," Dan suggested, hoping his voice was just at the right level of buddy-buddy effect, so the other man would be put at ease.

Carl stared into Dan's eyes, a strange expression on his face. "Didn't Ruby tell you?"

"Just a little. She was afraid that...well I don't know what. But she didn't say much. Just that you were off to some lost continent."

Carl laughed, his face distorting in humor. "That lost continent thing...that really over-simplifies it! Not really so simple as that!"

His voice became serious as he continued. "At one time it *was* a lost continent, I guess. But not now. All that's left—at this point anyway—is a little tropical island, which I don't believe is even marked on the maps. On that island is a temple—mostly in ruins, from what I've been able to tell from my uncle's notes. There are ruins around the temple. What has made it stand there for so long, I don't know. But it still stands. And in it is something of...well, great value. Uncle called it *The Virgin Venus...*"

"But where did it all come from?" Dan wanted to know, more interested than he wished to admit.

"At one time, so the story goes, there was a continent that spanned most of the Pacific Ocean. And on it was the birthplace of the human race. This was the original Garden of Eden. There are records of this place all over the world, if you know how to really read the records.

"They're told in symbols and things like that. It's even believed that...I'm not sure...but that Noah was part of the—well, you know the story. The world was supposed to have sunk—or been flooded...Oh, hell, I can't think right now. I don't believe it was Noah. I really don't know. It *must* have been far back even before his time. Maybe some earlier version upon which the Biblical Noah was fashioned. I've even heard of a mythological place called Haldolen—the Haldolen Empire, which was supposed to have existed some thirty to forty thousand years ago, centered in the Pacific Ocean and spread out across the world. Pre-Columbian Mesoamerica may have been the result of its early colonies...well, it is all Howdy Doody Land. I mean, give me a break. All fantasy island hocus po-cus. Nobody really knows. Just theories. And damned to theories. All that counts is reality.

"But anyway there was this continent, more re-cently dubbed Mu, which one day suddenly went bang! Exploded. Apparently—so the tale goes—it was located on a series of gas pockets which sud-denly exploded, and then up went the whole caboo-dle. The survivors fled in all directions at once. Be-fore it sank, though, there was supposed to be a vast civilization spanning the whole world. Again, fits the Haldolen Empire tripe! The Mayans and the In-cas and all that were supposed to have been started by this race of people. The South Sea Islanders are believed to be descendents of the race. They went East, too.

"Anyway, it's all a beautiful, if silly theory. And that's all it is. The fact is that there is an island with a temple on it, with a *Fire Venus Idol* in it! Beyond that, I don't know much, except that our uncle seemed to believe there was some kind of curse on

the island. On the temple. And on *The Virgin Venus.*
A lot of rot gut, but I don't give a damn! Money is
money.

"And there's supposed to be more than any
thousand people could spend in a thousand years if
they threw it away! I don't know—but..." Carl
paused and then said, "Give me another drink—and
let's talk about something different!"

"What?" Dan asked, handing the rum over.

"Women—girls—sex! Anything!" Carl gulped
the rum and then wiped his lips with the back of his
hand. "What you think of Ruby?"

The question was so direct and so unexpected
that Dan didn't have an answer for several seconds.
Then he finally said, "She's quite a woman!"

Carl smiled and his eyes gleamed. "I've heard
better reports than that about my dear little sister,"
he said.

"Like what?"

"You should know better than me. But just to let
you in on it...I sometimes wish I were in your shoes.
Brother! To have a woman like Ruby that I could
bed! I've tried to find one—but if there *is* another
I've not found her!"

It seemed strange to Dan, to be talking about
Carl's sister in such a way. He shrugged and then
said, "Like I told you—she's quite a woman!"

Ruby's voice broke in on their conversation:
"So you think I'm quite a woman, do you?"

Dan turned, startled, not knowing what to say.

Carl blurted out: "Speak of the devil and here
she comes!"

Ruby's eyes flared at her brother and then she
turned to Dan. "I think Billy Turk wants you on

deck."

"What?"

"Come along," she urged, taking hold of his hand and pulling.

Carl started to follow them out the door, but Ruby held him back with her other hand. "Stay, Carl!"

She whispered in Dan's ear: "I want to see you—*alone!*"

Dan shrugged and followed Ruby out to the corridor and up to the deck.

CHAPTER SEVEN

Ruby led him over to the far side of the boat, away from where Billy Turk was, and then she turned and looked up into his eyes, her expression very serious. "I wanted to talk about where we are heading. Tell you what you're in for. Then you can make up your mind on what you want to do. You know there will be some danger to what we're do-ing—where we're going. And I think it's only fair to tell you—to let you know."

"Nice of you to tell me," he said in a dull voice. "But your brother already said something about where we're going!"

"Then you know all about it?"

"A little," he admitted. "He said something about curses and things like that. But I don't believe in the supernatural."

"It's not the supernatural I'm worried about," Ruby said in a serious voice. "There are some men after Carl. For money that he owes them. They know about the island and what's on the island. That's why we had to leave in a hurry."

"I figured there was something the matter last night."

"I'm sorry about not being with you," she told him in a low, rasping voice. "But I had to talk a few things over with Carl—and do a little nursing."

"I'd like a dear little nurse like you," Dan told her.

Ruby smiled and then brushed back a lock of dark hair. "Then you don't mind being pushed into this?"

"Who pushed?" he offered somewhat lightly.

"I guess I did, maybe a little—well...you know what I mean!" Ruby paused and then said, "You can be paid a flat amount—or take a cut in the find!"

Dan thought that one over, and then decided that if there were others interested in what Ruby was headed for, then there must be a lot of money involved. "I'll take a cut."

"One percent!" Ruby offered.

"You kidding? Thirty percent."

"A third! Oh, no," she objected. "Ten—and that's it!"

"Okay—on one condition: at least fifty thousand." Ruby thought that over and then nodded. "That's fair enough. The Venus Idol should be worth a little over ten million dollars—from what my uncle said! But what happens if it all turns out to be no dice—if nothing happens? What if the island isn't even there?"

"I'll take it out on your bod!" Dan laughed. "Fair enough?"

Ruby laughed and then said: "That's a deal breaker—the only thing is that *I* get a lot out of it that way, too. I almost hope we don't find anything!"

"Don't say that!" he warned in a stage whisper, looking nervously from side to side as if there were a huge audience surrounding them.

She laughed at that, punching him lightly on the chest in a loving way.

The ocean breeze was whipping her dark hair around her face and it gave her a deliciously savage look.

"What's the time of arrival?" he asked, becoming serious again. "You haven't even told me how far we are to go."

"Tomorrow, if we make time. Just keep to the course I gave you last night."

"Billy will do just that until I tell him differently."

Dan looked at his watch. It was a little less than an hour before he was supposed to take the wheel. He looked up at Ruby again, his eyes meeting hers. "I have a little time."

"For what?"

"Guess."

She took his hand and led him toward the cabins, below deck.

* * * * * * *

Billy Turk watched the ocean and the sun. The day was beginning to turn to noon, and Dan Shon hadn't appeared for his break at the wheel.

It's that woman witch, Billy thought angrily. *She's cast a spell on Matie Dan!*

Billy turned his thoughts from Dan to Miss West. He tried to think about the last woman he had had. A prostitute in one of the houses on the island. A coarse woman, but the kind he liked. Full and large. Wide-hipped and sluttish. That had been almost a week ago, and he didn't like the idea of being away from a woman for so long.

Taking a deep breath, Billy looked out on the deck and was surprised to see Ruby West standing there looking up at him.

"Mind if I join you?" she called.

"Sure, Miss—come on up!"

Ruby moved like a sensual cat as she stepped up the ladder and then glided toward him. For a long time she stood staring at Billy and then observed:

"You haven't decided if you like me, have you, Billy?"

"What's makin' you think that?" he asked, feeling uncomfortable, trying to avoid her eyes.

"Oh, a woman can tell!" He didn't say anything. "You've known Dan long?"

"For several years."

"Been working for him all that time?"

"Mostly."

Silence.

The wind blew across the ocean, whipping up little waves, which tossed the ship. Billy had to correct course.

"Windy, isn't it," Ruby commented, leaning closer to Billy.

"A little."

"Think it will storm?"

Billy felt that uneasiness again. He wished she would go and leave him, or that Dan would come up and take over the wheel.

"I don't think it'll storm."

"Did the other night."

A heavy, leaden silence fell on them, and then Billy asked: "Is Dan in his cabin?"

"No!" was Ruby's simple and direct answer.

"Where?"

"In *my* cabin!" The way she said it sounded bluntly possessive. "Sleeping, I believe!"

"He was supposed to take over," Billy told her.

"Oh—you've been at the wheel for quite a while, then?" she asked, concern shading her voice.

"A spell."

"I could take over."

"No—Dan wouldn't like that!" Billy said in a firm, unshakable voice.

For a long time there was a silence and then Ruby asked, almost in a childlike voice. "What kind of man is Dan Shon, really?"

The question startled Billy, because he was sure that Ruby knew exactly what kind of a man he was.

Billy thought that over and then said: "Dan's had a hard life and lives hard. He fights hard and he loves hard. He's a good pal and a good buddy. He's a man that don't take nothin' from nobody—and he'll just as easily kill to protect a lady's honor. He's a good man, that too many women like yourself takes after and takes advantage!"

Billy broke off, startled with what he had said.

Ruby cried, "I was right about you! You *don't* like me!"

"That's not so. I don't think you're good for Dan—that's all!"

"The same thing!" Ruby announced in an amused voice. "The same thing, Billy Turk! But maybe you're wrong!"

It was a long time before either of them said anything, and then Ruby finally stepped away, offering:

"Well, I'll go get Dan and tell him it's his turn

at the wheel!" As she stepped down to the lower deck she called over her shoulder: "That make you like me better—you old witch doctor?"

Billy Turk was startled to hear Ruby refer to him as a witch doctor.

"You go get Dan—tell him to get himself up here!"

Angrily he shrugged his gigantic shoulders.

A little while later Dan Shon stepped on deck, moved over to Billy and took over the wheel.

CHAPTER EIGHT

Slowly the small boat moved across the ocean to Tellbrooke Island. On board were two Americans. Anna Terrie and Jim Gordon. Anna was sunning on the deck, a bottle of rum sitting near the towel she was lying on. She was resting, trying to blot out the evening before. It had been messy and dirty.

Gordon had come into their cabin, and after getting himself completely plastered he'd abused the hell out of her in every possible way.

Gordon is a gross bastard! She thought savagely, trying to hold down the bitterness in her. *One of these days she'd be rid of men like him. One of these days she would be free to kick them right in the balls.*

There had been too many Jim Gordons in her life. From small farm girl to big city girl in a few easy lessons. A man had come to work on her folks' farm, dated and daringly seduced her. She'd run after him when he left. The man had used her for a long time before dumping her. Other men took his place. One after another. She'd managed to survive by using her body—luckily she enjoyed sex. And enjoyed men.

For now it was Jim Gordon, and maybe a big wad of money. She'd take that away from him. She hated Gordon—and all the other Gordons in her past. All she had wanted as a young girl was a happy home, a child and a good husband—and the only thing she had gotten was one bastard after another.

Anna sighed and rolled over on her stomach, reached for the bottle of rum and pulled the top out. Raising the bottleneck to her lips, she gulped thirstily. The liquor felt good to her insides.

They were two days out to sea and no end to the ocean. She hated the ocean and she hated everybody on board. Gordon had hired a couple of toughs from the docks and then rented a boat. It was a seedy and sorry crew.

"Miss Torrie!" a man's low, gruff voice sounded from behind her.

Anna looked around. It was one of the new men. Derk something. He had a black, heavy beard and his eyes were deep-set. There was a hardness about him; cruel, like Jim Gordon.

"What do you want?" she asked, holding back the contempt she felt for the man.

"The master wants to see you!"

"What about?" Anna asked. "What does the *master* bastard want?"

"You! In the cabin! Come!" Derk squinted at Anna and then jerked his head toward the companionway.

Slowly Anna stood and then stepped past the man. She didn't like the way he looked at her figure. The bikini showed a lot of her body, and she suddenly felt naked to his gaze. There was open heat in his eyes. Little crawling sensations ran up and down her back like insects having a holiday.

Anna shook herself and stepped down into the companionway, then to the small cabin. She opened the door and stepped in. "What you want, Gordy?"

"Don't you call me that!" the man commanded, twisting his ugly face in a snarl. The scar on his right cheek shaped into an L as his lips slowly re-shaped to an ugly smile. "You're dressed good, Anna!"

She didn't say anything to that—just stared at him. Gordon was dressed in a clean white shirt and safari pants. There was a holster on the chair with an ugly-looking black Luger.

"You shouldn't dress like that for Derk and Jake. They might not like it. Or rather like it too much for your own good."

"What do you want?"

"You—that's all! Tomorrow we should be at the island. Then all we gotta do is spot the others. Then we're set for life. All the way, little one!"

"Go to hell!" she snapped, angered by his attitude. She didn't know exactly what it was that bothered her. "What do you want?"

"Come here and find out!"

"Not right now!" she told him firmly.

Gordon stared at Anna for a short moment and then, before she even realized what was happening, he leaped forward, gripped her in one hand and slapped the other across her face.

The pain of the blow numbed Anna so that she wasn't aware of Gordon's hands ripping aside her bikini, first at the top and then at the bottom. When she realized what had happened she instinctively whipped out a hand, smashing it across the man's face.

Gordon stared at her for a moment, and then a sharp intake of breath sucked from his thin lips.

"You damned bitching whore! You damned bitchin' whore!" he screamed.

Anna felt a hard fist bury itself in her stomach. A terrible, unexpected blow that left her dizzy with agony. She felt herself double over.

Then another blow smashed into her face. It stunned her as she gasped for breath. Her whole insides were bursting in fiery torture. She felt herself being lifted and then dropped on a bunk. Then there was a moment's pause and she felt a heavy body climb down on her.

Still the breath didn't come back to her lungs.

"I'll teach you—you bitch!" a rasping voice hissed in her ear. "Teach you to jump!"

Suddenly her breasts were being brutally caressed with teeth and lips. She was helpless, unable to protect herself from his cruel and savage attack.

The hurt of him on her, and the biting agony of his teeth and lips continued until the red haze changed abruptly to heated passion. Her own nerves and body responded as he suddenly entered her with one savage thrust. She felt her body squirming and thrusting up against Gordon's, greedily taking him into her.

She felt him claw at her as his body surged and continued to hammer at her. They became one lunging rhythm that ravished them through the last stages of passion. She hated him for making her like it. She hated the instant, automatic response her body gave to that man's brutal attack

* * * * * * *

It was morning again, and Dan was finding it hard to break the haze of hangover from his head.

He was drinking too much—too hard. He had to bring an end to the long drunken binge.

It seemed as if his brain wasn't working at all. It seemed as if he were still under some kind of supernatural spell. He couldn't shake the feeling—he couldn't help himself either. Slowly he slid from the bunk, careful not to wake Ruby, who was still sleeping.

Quickly getting dressed, he stepped out of the cabin and then moved to the galley, a small nook with a little stove and a small table. He fixed coffee and while it was heating he stepped out on deck, where Billy Turk was standing by the wheel.

"How's it going, Billy?" he asked, exploring the horizon with his eyes.

"Island straight ahead. Just at the horizon, matie!"

Dan stared, but it was a long time before he spotted the small dot. "Think that's the place?"

"Don't know, matie. According to what I was told by … by them."

They were silent and then Dan nodded to Billy, "Coffee should be ready pretty soon. So help yourself, I'll take over."

When he was alone, Dan felt a sense of power. The sea worked its own spell over his depressed hangover.

Ever since he had come to the South Seas he'd fallen in love with the waters and the calm. There was something about it that relaxed the soul and quieted the spirit. It was as if God's hand had rested on the waters and then said that this was his haven of peace, and anybody who moved upon it would find rest of soul and cleansing of spirit.

Nothing could touch you at sea, except a storm, but that seldom happened. He wanted the sea and he wanted the peace it offered to his troubled mind.

Ruby's voice interrupted his thoughts. "Hello!" she greeted, stepping up to him and patting his shoulder.

Turning, Dan looked at her, feeling a sense of tenderness toward her. In the morning there was something childlike about Ruby, with none of the mystifying strangeness of her when she was the exotic woman who could cast him under her fiery web of passion and make him melt into her arms—and willing to do anything she might ask. Now she was only a woman—very beautiful and very desirable.

"You're a strange one, Ruby!"

"How's that?" she asked in an innocent voice.

"In one way you're like a little child. In another you're a strange and almost terrifying woman," Dan told her, keeping his eyes on the distant dot on the horizon.

Ruby didn't say anything to that, only remained silently standing beside him.

"See that dot out there?" Dan asked, pointing to the horizon.

Ruby stared for a moment and then a sharp intake of breath told Dan what he wanted to know. But she put it in words.

"That's Tellbrooke! It has to be!" she exclaimed in excitement. Then, moving away from him to the small stairway, she cried: "I'll have to wake Carl. To tell him!" Then she disappeared.

Dan stood there, gazing at the distant island and thinking that there lay his destiny. He couldn't help thinking that. He couldn't help feeling that what took place on the island would change his whole life.

A chill ran down his spine as he watched the dot grow larger and larger.

There was his destiny!

CHAPTER NINE

The island was surrounded by high cliffs, against which the ocean splashed its huge watery arms, helplessly attempting to wash them away. There was a heavy mist surrounding the cliffs, hiding their upper portions so that Dan Shon couldn't tell if they mightn't rise a thousand miles above the earth's surface. He stood at the wheel of the *Sea Witch,* following the cliffs in search for an opening.

There was a strange silence broken only by the waves in their attack on the cliffs. It seemed as if they had come to the end of the world they knew, and once they made contact with the island they would find themselves in another alien planet, evil and filled with unknown horrors. He couldn't get the feeling out of his mind.

"It's enough to scare even the gods, matie," Billy Turk said in a low, awe-filled voice. "I don't like it none!"

"An island is an island—nothing more!" Dan exclaimed. But somehow his words had a hollow sound to them, lacking conviction.

"What you make of it?" Billy asked.

"What?"

"The sound. Nothing. Just the ocean!"

"We're too far away to know what sounds might

61

be coming from the island."

Carl West stepped up to Dan and said: "There's supposed to be an opening on the northeast end. That's what my uncle's manuscript says."

"Well, we're almost there!" Dan told the younger man, hiding the irritation he felt for Carl. There was something about Ruby's brother that bothered him. Maybe it was because Dan couldn't help feeling that Carl was a bloody coward.

Carl West was small of build and had an innocent, inexperienced appearance to his face. And a weak chin. Then there was the way he had talked about his sister. The man had the hots for Rita. At least that's what it had sounded like to Dan. Even if it was true he shouldn't be sharing such thoughts about his own sister!

"Did your uncle say anything about what's on the island?" Dan asked, guiding the boat around the rocky bend.

"Jungle—at least that's what the manuscript says."

"Nothing more?"

"The Temple of Mu...that's what he called it...is on a rocky grade leading to the mountains. Surrounded by a swamp. That's just about all I know—except for a map which tells the way to the temple, through the swamp."

"Sounds lovely!"

"Sounds frightnin' to me, matie!" Billy whispered. "I don't like it none. Not at all!"

Dan continued to keep his eyes alert for any break in the endless cliffs that made up the outside of the island. "Any natives or anything on the island?"

"I don't know! Uncle didn't say. I don't think so." Ruby's voice shouted from the front of the boat where she had been leaning over the rail, looking for the opening to the island. "There it is! Over to your right!" Her voice was high with excitement.

Dan's eyes moved along the cliff line and spotted a series of rocks broken away from the overhang and surrounding a small opening in them.

"That's going to be one hell of a squeeze!" Dan cursed under his breath, turning the boat in that direction. For a long time they continued forward at full speed, and then Dan shut off the motor and let the little *Sea Witch* slow continue on its course. "Billy, take a look!"

Billy Turk rushed forward and a moment later returned grinning. "The gods are with you! It's an easy one. Deep as hell! Just keep away from the damned rocks!"

"Keep a look out!"

Billy returned to the front of the boat and kept calling out directions.

It seemed for Dan as though a hundred years clawed their slow way in those short moments. The ocean was beginning to get choppier, and the danger of being swept onto the rocks was enough to make his stomach twist up inside him like an eggbeater with spikes.

But slowly the cliffs moved closer, and he started the motor again, creeping slowly, ready to shift it to a quick reverse if necessary. But the sailing was smooth right to the end.

As they slipped from the ocean to the inner curve of the cliffs, Dan felt his breath suddenly bolt out of his lungs in relief. They were moving into a perfect land-locked lagoon, but what startled him was the small pier at the far end of the lagoon.

"Billy! Take over!" Dan shouted. The moment Turk was beside him, Dan rushed off for his cabin and opened his gun case. The little pier didn't promise trouble and it didn't even promise people, but there wasn't any reason to take unnecessary chances—and he didn't plan on taking them. It wasn't natural. And it wasn't all that ancient.

Dan picked out a long-nosed .38 pistol for himself, tucking it in his belt and a high-powered rifle for Billy. For a moment he thought about giving Carl and Ruby weapons, and then decided against it. Taking another two pistols, he placed a small .38 in his right pocket and then took an Army .45 for Billy. If anything happened that they needed to have weapons all around, then he could hand out the extra weapons.

After picking up several boxes of bullets, Dan returned to the deck and handed Billy the .45 and the rifle.

"Just in case," he said.

They were almost to the dock and Dan saw that it was older than he'd thought and broken down. The dock wasn't more than ten yards long and several boards were rotted away.

"It's been some time since the builders were around," he observed.

Ruby nodded.

Billy said: "But not that long!"

The woman said: "Maybe our uncle built it."

Nobody said anything to that. They were all gazing at their surroundings and for the first time Dan took notice. The lagoon was bordered on all sides with thick tropical jungle. The green of the underbrush was spotted with vivid splashes of color, ranging from bright red to purple, yellow and orange.

The chirp of jungle birds and the distant cry of what Dan was sure must be a big jungle cat, seemed to bring a warmth to the island. From the ocean it all had seemed dreadfully quiet and terrifying, but now it was simply a part of the tropical earth. Still, a shiver ran through Dan.

Then he realized what it was that was bothering him. There shouldn't be any big jungle cats in the South Seas! Not here, at least. The shiver iced down his spine.

Billy Turk guided the *Sea Witch* up to the dock and Dan jumped out, tying the boat to one of the pillars that stuck to the bottom of the lagoon.

"You'll have to be careful!" Dan shouted to the others. The dock was broken and holed with rotted gray beams. Moss covered part of the boards where their broken ends dipped into the clear blue waters. "I'll check it out!"

Carefully Dan took a testing step forward, placing his foot gently in front of him, before giving it his full weight. One step followed another, and he was surprised to discover that the boards that still stood were sturdy, holding under his weight. "If they hold up Billy—they'll hold up anybody!"

"Be right with you, matie!" Billy shouted, leaping over the bow of the ship and plunking his weight on the dock. A broad grin spread across his face and for the first time in days his eyes were twinkling with the excitement of a new adventure.

It was the old Billy Turk with whom Dan had

gone through some tough times. Billy, the man who fought with both fists and wasn't afraid of devil or man. The gun had done its job well on Billy's mental attitude. His bulky weight didn't have any more effect on the solid boards than Dan's lighter pounds. "Seems solid to me, matie!"

"Okay, Ruby, Carl!" Dan called to the others.

"Come along, we'll take a look around."

Dan stepped down from the dock and then moved to the sandy, short beach. The jungle sounds around him seemed to get quieter, as if the island had suddenly become aware of strangers entering its domain. That old shiver settled down his spine and he shook it off, turning to watch the others join him. After they had come up to him, he stared from one to the other.

Finally he said in a slow, careful voice: "I don't know how you plan on proceeding from here but I have several ideas. One is to look around the general area surrounding the lagoon and then staying here for the night so that we can get a fresh start in the morning."

Carl's face contorted into a frown. "*What the hell!* Why can't we get started right away? What's keeping us? I want to get there as fast as possible!"

"It's best that we find out exactly what we're up against!"

"What are you talking about?" Carl cried.

"I heard some kind of big cat in the jungle—and there's not supposed to be any such animal in this part of the world! At least not on a small island like this. So I would rather take a careful look around—first!"

Ruby stared strangely at Dan for a long moment,

her eyes becoming dark and deep, as if she were gazing into his inner mind. Finally she said: "Maybe you're right! We'll take a look and start out tomorrow!"

Then she added: "I think it's about time we showed you the manuscript anyway. Tonight after dinner!"

"Okay—that's settled!" announced Dan, relieved that Ruby had decided to go along with him.

"Hell, no!" Carl objected.

Ruby turned to her brother. "Look, Carl, another day won't make that much difference. The temple has waited all these years—so it can wait a little longer!"

After a moment Carl relaxed and then nodded.

"Okay—we'll do it your way this time, Dan!" There seemed to be a hidden threat in the man's voice. A tight, deep threat.

"Okay, then," Dan said. "Let's take a look around."

He led the way along the short, narrow, sandy white beach, keeping his eyes alert for any sign of possible danger. Dan had been in tropical jungles enough to know that the unexpected could be expected. He didn't want to take any unnecessary chances.

As they moved forward, the silence spread before them. It was the kind of silence, which comes before a storm, waiting and ready to burst out with lightning death from nowhere.

Dan felt cold sweat cover his body and his hand instinctively moved to the .38 in his belt. Something about the silence warned him; something about the way it settled over the surrounding jungle—all of it all at once.

He paused and the others did the same.

He had come to the end of the sandy stretch of beach, where the jungle undergrowth moved to the lagoon waters. A bush rustled in front of Dan, and he found his hand gripping the pistol's handle, slowly pulling it out.

Then, as the bushes parted and the cry of a leopard broke the silence, Dan's hand flew up, aiming the small .38 pistol at the cat, automatically, without thinking how useless it was against such an animal.

He pulled the trigger three times. The leopard jerked but didn't pause once in its charge directly at him.

CHAPTER TEN

There was an explosion from behind Dan just as the leopard's body flew through the air, directly at his head. For a moment time seemed to stand still—and then he felt the impact of the cat's form smash into him, knocking his body to the ground.

For a stunned moment he waited for the curving talons to carve his stomach to shredded meat. It seemed an eternity, as he lay there dazed and unable to move. Then suddenly he was aware of voices.

He's not dead?" Ruby cried in fear.

"Dan! Damn it all, matie!" Billy shouted.

Dan heard a moan and then realized the sound came from his own throat. It was several moments before he could move. Then slowly he started to struggle from under the leopard, which he now realized must be dead.

"Here, let's help him!" Billy said, as Dan felt the man's strong hands slide under his arms and pull him to his feet. "You all right, matie?"

Dan stood, supported by the heavy seaman, trying to clear his head and shake the numbness now settling over it. "That...that...was...too close," he managed, opening his eyes for the first time.

"I thought you were—dead!" Ruby whispered in a low, frightened voice.

"He would have been, too, if Billy hadn't acted!" Carl pointed out in an awed tone.

Dan looked down at the dead leopard and then at Billy. Smiling weakly, he nodded. "That's one for you, Billy!"

"Think nothin' of it, matie! You've saved my skin a little in the past!"

For only a moment longer did they stand there, and then Ruby suggested they return to the boat. "You've had enough for today, I think!"

Dan Shon stared at her for a moment and then shook his head. "Not enough. We'll do better to look things over a little first and then return. But you two stay close by us—just in case something like that happens again."

Turning, Dan stepped into the underbrush from which the leopard had sprung. A series of questions was running in his mind. One of them being: What was a leopard doing on an island like this? It didn't figure. But then, nothing had figured since he'd met Ruby West. Now, this island was just one more link in the chain of the strange and odd.

The others followed close behind him, each stepping carefully forward, as if expecting something deadly to pop out at them from any side. The heat of the sun burned down on their bodies like a hot flame. Dan could feel the sweat oiling his body.

After walking about twenty yards into the jungle undergrowth, he turned to the right, in the direction where they had left the boat.

"There's no need going too far. The thing I wanted to know, I've found out. This is going to take some cutting through, unless we can find some game trails."

70

As he spoke, he brushed a thick vine from the path in front of his face, and then stepped over a thick root sticking up from the ground, as if to accent his statement.

Sighing, Dan turned to the others. "We might as well turn back. Get to the ship. You can show me the manuscript, and let me have some idea in what direction we have to go tomorrow."

They walked through the jungle for several minutes longer before reaching the white sandy beach.

Then directly to the boat. Once in the galley, Dan told Carl to bring the manuscript. He got out a quart of rum and some glasses.

"I could use somethin' like that, matie!" Billy Turk exclaimed.

By the time Carl had returned with a bulky package, the others had already had several sips of rum and were beginning to relax after the close call with the leopard.

Carl sat at the table next to Dan and unwrapped the package, exposing an old manuscript.

"Tell me something about your uncle, Carl," Dan said. "What kind of man was he?"

"A strange one."

"That doesn't tell me much!" Dan snapped angrily.

Ruby broke in with: "Uncle Frank was the kind of man who saw everything in black and white. Good and evil. He wasn't really such a good scientist. Really it was only a hobby with him. He had money and used it to explore regions that gave indication of lost cities. Or what he thought might be. He was somewhat of a foolish dreamer, if you ask me."

"But," her brother pointed out, "not such a silly fool as some people thought!"

She continued with: "He believed in the theory of the Lost Continent of Mu. Usually he was laughed at for believing in it. The generous ones said it this thing had any value it was only for its very age. Since the Mu thing has always been considered eighteenth-century bunk, they simply shrugged their shoulders and mocked him with silly grins. Well, that's the way he kept telling it. This manuscript was the only evidence he had, to prove his theory. Some scientists looked over parts of it— just a little—since he wouldn't let the location of the island be known to anybody. The end result was their mockery. He had some idea that there was something supernatural about this island and what he had found here. Maybe his secrecy kept much of the facts from those he talked to in the scientific world. Anyway, he was a strange man."

Carl nodded: "Bloody strange!"

"Well, anyway, those that looked at his findings, photos of writings on the walls of the temple, claimed it was only a primitive civilization. Nothing more. But they were vastly interested in seeing it. Uncle Frank wouldn't have any of that. Finally he clammed up about it. He just claimed there was danger here."

"And," Carl broke in, "that what he had found would shock mankind!"

"Do you think he was wrong?"

Carl shook his head: "We wouldn't be here, if we thought he was. A dead city is a dead city— that's all. That's all that we know about it or care to believe about it.

"But there's a huge Venus Idol in the temple, which has rubies and emeralds and things like that...diamonds. The Venus Idol is made of gold, according to Uncle."

Carl paused and then added, a greedy glow in his eyes: "That's what we're after—and that's the only thing we're after!"

Dan shrugged. "Continue..."

"Look at the manuscript—page 35—there's a map there," Carl suggested.

Dan turned the old pages of paper and found page 35. It seemed the same as the others.

"Read from the top!"

Dan read:

> ...And you go through the jungle, which is like a mass of evil trapped in the middle of the cliff walls. Go northeast from Circle Cove, for about two miles. There you reach the beginning slopes of the mountain...and the beginning of the ruins. Continue through until you reach the temple. You can't miss it.

Dan paused and looked up, moving his eyes from one to another.

Then he looked down at the manuscript again and continued reading:

> In order to get into the temple, you have to enter through the huge doorway. Be careful not to touch anything

on the entrance. It might trigger off some hidden device which will send an arrow of death through the man touching it!

Dan paused and then said: "He writes this as if—like directions..."

"At this point he was planning on telling his discovery to the world," Carl pointed out. Then he added: "There's nothing on that page of importance at all, from that point. I can tell you the basic story from there.

"Uncle went into the temple, found most of it in ruins and found several devices which were set to kill anybody who might try to enter the temple. The amazing thing about it was that they worked. How long they had been there he didn't know—but he guessed it must have been thousands of years."

"That's impossible!" Dan shouted.

"Witchcraft!" Billy Turk said in an awed voice. There was a note of fear to the word.

"Don't be silly, that's just a lot of island crap!" Dan snapped, flashing his eyes toward Billy. "There's no such thing as witchcraft. At least not in reality. The only reality it has is what your mind gives it!"

"You're wrong, matie!" Billy told him in a solemn voice.

"Continue, Carl!" Dan told the younger man.

"Well—Uncle broke down as many traps as he could find, and then carefully explored the ruins. After that, he discovered a passage down below the surface of the ground.

"There is where he found this Venus Idol. He

74

called it *The Virgin Venus* because it was shaped in the form of a very beautiful naked woman. Young and innocent. He took photographs of it—but we couldn't find any when we went through his things."

"How do you know that it really exists?" Dan demanded, suddenly beginning to think that maybe their uncle was just some crackpot.

"If you knew him, you'd know it was true! That was good enough for me."

"He could have been off his head. Maybe from the jungle—fever hits people."

"That wasn't it. There were others that saw it all, too. Most of them are dead. Only one survived. But he died in prison. So..."

"So maybe it was all made up!" Dan exploded. "Why wouldn't he bring it up? Why wouldn't he—I mean...return to the island?"

"He believed in hocus pocus. He had his evidence!"

"What?'

Carl didn't say anything for a long time and then he just shrugged his shoulders. "Maybe we'd better find out for ourselves!"

Anger flushed through Dan. He half stood, glaring at Carl. "I'll find out in the manuscript—so why hold that information back?"

Carl just smiled at him: "Don't be silly! I destroyed those parts. I didn't see any reason to keep them."

Billy Turk cursed under his breath and then slammed his heavy fist against the table. "Stupid, stupid!"

All eyes turned to Billy.

"We could've known what we're up against!"

"If you believe in that," Carl pointed out coldly, "then you can always stay here on the boat!"

Dan laughed. "Come on, guys. The only thing to be nervous about is people with guns who are out to get you. The supernatural is just that. Nonsense. So knock it off, Billy."

Billy stared in heated anger at the other men for a long time.

Dan continued: "The main thing is that we get started on this and then—we'll see...the rest of you must have something to do—I'll study the manuscript and then we'll leave early tomorrow morning.

"Billy, you get things in order here—and...hell, better arm everybody—we don't know what we'll find in the jungle—and there's no reason we should take any chances!"

For only a moment the others stood there motionless, and then they moved from the room one at a time. Dan turned his attention to the manuscript, feeling a combination of excitement and a strange inner threat of anxiety about what he read.

He passed over the details concerning the day-by-day record of their exploration of the ruined city. It had several gaps. All that Dan could make out from reading was that several men were killed—but there wasn't any explanation. Finally he discovered the passage which described The Virgin Venus. He read it over several times:

> Ten feet tall and golden. Inlaid with jewels of every kind. Beautifully shaped. Tall and slender. Youthful. The expression on her face is that of innocence. That's the reason I have dubbed

it The Virgin Venus.

It was late at night when Dan finally fell exhausted into his bunk, his eyes blurred and aching from reading. He had discovered little about the ruins and about the island, beyond what he had already guessed or been told. No explanation about the leopards. Only mention of them, but no theories about their existence on the island.

His brain and body were exhausted, to the point where every nerve felt on fire. The moment he hit the bed, he felt sleep dropping over his mind, bringing quick unconsciousness.

With sleep came the black of nightmares.

In his unconscious mind came the image of a tall virgin Venus Idol suddenly swaying and then move. Its arms reached out toward him, the smiling golden face became mobile, the lips pursing into a sensual kiss.

"Come to me...!" was its hollow invitation.

But when Dan tried to move toward the living Idol, he found that his legs couldn't take a step.

He couldn't budge a muscle.

Then suddenly he was sitting up in bed, sweat breaking from every pore. His nerves felt like they were shaking, but his hand was steady.

For a long time he stared at the top of his small cabin. Then slowly he forced himself to relax and then looked at his watch. It was eight in the morning.

Dan moved from the bunk. His mind was at the bottom of a deep well of depression.

Sighing, he got dressed, and then stepped out onto deck. For about ten minutes he sat there, staring at the jungle, trying to calm his nerves. Then finally he turned and went below deck. It was time to get the others up—they had to start out.

But even as he began waking the others, he could not but wonder what they were going to find out on that mountainside. What hidden horrors. Or would it all turn out to be just simply a ruined city, which had once housed a primitive race of people who had built a golden statue to worship?

He didn't know—and he was almost afraid to find out. But there wasn't anything that he could do about it.

By nine o'clock they were stepping from the boat, each armed with a pistol and a rifle. Each silent and grim. It was as if all seemed to feel the same sense of impending danger in the next few hours.

CHAPTER ELEVEN

They had gone around the island three times before Jim Gordon spotted the only opening in the cliffs. "That must be the only entrance! That has to be!" he exclaimed. "Head for it!"

Slowly the boat changed course and then needled its way toward the little opening in the huge cliffs. The morning sun was hot on the waters and the sweat was dripping from Gordon's body as if it was a wet sponge.

As they entered the gap between the cliffs splattered with barren, jagged rocks, Gordon felt the hairs on the back of his neck raise with fear. "Be careful!" he shouted at Jake, who was at the wheel. "We don't want to be killed!"

Finally they made it past the opening and floated into the small lagoon.

"There they are!" Gordon shouted, pointing. He pulled out the Luger from its holster at his side. Checking the weapon, then turning to the others, he called to them softly, "Be ready for a fight. Shoot to kill! I don't want any of them alive!"

Anna Torrie, who was now standing beside him, stared in shock at Gordon. "You're kidding!"

"Go to hell, Anna!" he snapped angrily. "We don't want them getting in our way!"

Slowly the boat moved toward the *Sea Witch.*
Gordon kept his eyes sharply alert for any sign of
life on the other boat, but didn't find any.

"They're not home!" he observed, "but be careful! Might be a trap!"

Finally they were sliding alongside the *Sea
Witch,* and Derk was the first to board her. After
him Gordon jumped to the boat. Silently the two
men stepped along the deck. Then as they came to
the hatch leading below deck, Gordon motioned
Derk to open it.

Derk's muscular body tensed and then his foot
kicked out, hitting the hatch and swinging it in-
wards.

Both covered the opening.

Silence met them.

"Okay—easy does it!" Gordon said, directing
Derk to enter first.

"I'll cover you!" he said bravely.

The other man stepped carefully forward, his
small Luger pointed before him. He motion Gordon
to follow he said, "They've left!"

Quickly they went through the small cabins, and
then after having made sure there wasn't anybody
left on board, they stood in the companionway to
talk.

"We gotta go through the cabins. Find anything—maybe they left the information we want on
board!"

In the next twenty minutes they smashed
through every inch of the boat, and when they were
finished and sure there wasn't anything of value on
board, Gordon motioned to the other man.

"We'll sink her! They won't be needing this one

any longer, after we get through taking care of them!"

Gordon smiled evilly.

Derk laughed and then nodded.

It took the two of them a few minutes to open the extra gas cans stored in the *Sea Witch*. They spread the gas over the deck and then returned to their own boat. Gordon ordered Derk to light a match. For a moment the man started to object, then shrugged.

Gordon pushed the burning *Sea Witch* away from their boat and signaled Jake to reverse the engines. A moment later they were in the middle of the lagoon, watching the *Sea Witch* burn into the waters.

Afterwards they docked, climbed into a lifeboat and rowed to shore. It took only a few minutes to find the freshly cut trail which Dan Shon and the others had made a short time before.

* * * * * * *

Dan Shon had been cutting through the jungle underbrush for a little over twenty minutes when suddenly they came to a marsh, breaking the green of vines and the brown of tree trunks. The insects, which had been swarming around them from the moment they had started into the jungle suddenly seemed to dwindle. There was a strange silence before them. It seemed as if the jungle had suddenly become deceased and that even the air itself held death. There was a grayness to the marsh that moved before them. The few trees that spotted it were barren and bleak. A few hundred yards further, the marsh thickened and seemed to become swampy. There was an evil cast to everything that stretched before them.

Behind him he heard Ruby gasp in surprise.

"Looks like the gods been smellin' hate here, matie!" Billy whispered.

"Let's get going!" Carl ordered. "We can't stay here all day!"

Dan twisted his head to look at Carl. He didn't like the younger man. And the expression on the guy's face was open contempt and greed.

"Let's get going!" Carl shouted.

"Okay—okay!" Dan snapped, starting forward.

He sheathed the machete and lifted his rifle higher, ready for instant use. Carefully he moved forward, and then paused as the ground began to give way to water.

At first it was just moist ground, and then it started to become thicker with the beginnings of the swamp. "Be careful," he called to the others.

Carefully he took each step, testing the ground before him, making sure it wouldn't give way to beds of quicksand. There wasn't any way of knowing if each step would lead to death or not. He could feel an icy hand squeezing his body, wet with sweat. He didn't like this place.

To his right he heard a splashing sound. He turned and spotted a crocodile moving in their direction.

Quickly his gun flashed up. It flamed.

The water spurted at the side of the reptile.

Dan pulled the trigger once more. This time the bullet went to its mark, deep into the head of the crocodile.

Ruby screamed, terrified.

"Take it easy. It's all over!" Dan told her in a gentle voice, stepping forward again.

It was strange to Dan, the change that had come over Ruby in the last couple of days. It didn't seem like she had any supernatural power over him any more. It was as if she was just a little girl, helpless and innocent. A sexy body that knew how to make love to a man. But nothing else more magical.

He felt silly, having believed differently. Maybe the reality of the swamp was making him see things differently. He didn't know.

Dan's hand slapped up at an insect. "Damn!" he cursed.

Suddenly the ground under his feet seemed to give slightly. He felt panic flush through him. Desperately he threw his weight backwards, falling toward Ruby. Her body steadied him, and then he carefully pulled his foot out of the muddy waters and took a step back.

His arm wiped the sweat from his forehead. His eyes flashed around and spotted a tree branch a few feet from his head.

Taking his machete out, he chopped the branch until it came free from the tree. After trimming it and cutting it to a length of five feet, Dan then extended the short wooden pole forward, sticking it into the ground in front of him. The shaft sank deep, and continued to sink.

"Quicksand! We gotta be careful!" he said stiffly, moving the stick to his right. It was several seconds before he found a solid spot. Then for the next five minutes they were inching their way along, until they had passed the quicksand bed. After that he was careful to feel his way with the wooden shaft.

There was a light mist on the floor of the swamp now, and the waters came up to their knees. Progress was slow at first, but finally a sense of security came over Dan, and he felt sure they had bypassed the quicksand area. But nonetheless he was careful. Finally the swamp began to get shallow and then after a few minutes it dwindled out and they found themselves on solid ground once more.

"Thank God for that, matie!" Billy exclaimed, heaving a sigh of relief.

As they moved forward into the new, dry territory, the jungle they had left behind began to return, but this time not so thickly matted with undergrowth.

They moved boldly forward into the green and brown of the undergrowth, finding it possible to make their way without resorting to the machete. As they moved deeper, the jungle slowly began to come to life around them. The chirping of tropical birds was like a gentle concert to Dan's ears, lifting his depression away from him like a soothing hand.

The ground began rising, moving gently upwards as the undergrowth began to thin. Finally there were only trees, and vines twining around multicolored tropical flowers. Everything seemed to have turned into a paradise of life, bursting with sounds.

Then suddenly they stepped into a clearing, beyond which a rocky slope swelled upwards several yards, where it leveled out. They couldn't see beyond that.

"Well, at least it's more cheerful," Dan pointed

out.

"Thanks for that!" Ruby sighed, stepping to Dan's side.

Dan turned and looked at her for the first time since they had come out of the swamp. Her face was streaked with dirt, and her hair was wildly flowing over her shoulders. He couldn't help smiling. "You're quite a sight!"

"You should talk, Dan!" she smiled back, patting him on the cheek.

"Let's get going!" Carl urged impatiently.

Slowly they made their way up the rocky grade, moving between the huge boulders scattered in their passage. It was several minutes before they reached the top and by then Dan could feel the tiredness beginning to tell in his legs. It had been a long haul, and he didn't know how much farther they had to go.

It seemed as if they had walked for miles. The thick underbrush they had been forced to cut their way through, during the first hours, had sapped his body. Every muscle seemed to ache. The months of boozing had taken their toll on his strength, and now he was feeling the effects. Thought of liquor made his mouth dry, and he wished he'd taken some rum along.

As they stepped up to the top of the slope and onto level ground, they came to a startled stop.

Stretching out before them was a long expanse of what had once, maybe thousands of years before, been a city of some civilization which man had long ago forgotten. A long plain, speckled with crumbled buildings, broken walls, overgrown streets.

In the distance, against the mountainside serving

as the city's backdrop, was a large, impressive structure, topped by a strange and fearful figure in stone. Its face was that of a gigantic bird of evil, the eyes staring blankly out at them and its body that of a man, the arms stretching out, seeming to embrace the ruins surrounding it.

They had reached the lost city. They had found the temple in which, Dan knew now; he would find the proof of the existence of The Virgin Venus.

A shiver ran through Dan as he started forward, motioning the others to follow.

CHAPTER TWELVE

It was a city waiting through time, silently aging, slowly decaying away the splendor it once had known. The golden columns standing bold and broken to the sky, half-ghosts remaining of what had once been. A dead city—lost to man and lost to its own builders who died an unknown age ago. Standing alone and lonely, waiting for the hands of strangers.

They walked through the dirt paths overgrown with grasses and weeds. They walked silently, only the wind sighing in their ears.

The amazing thing was that the jungle hadn't covered these images like the Mayan ruins had been hidden by age and vegetation. Strangely, these seemed barren, much like those of Easter Island, only far more detailed, sophisticated.

Dan couldn't help feeling the excitement of an explorer treading on unknown land. It seemed as if the ghosts of a long-gone age still lived there in the ruins, laughing, loving, drinking, arguing the questions of all ages and all times.

What moral codes and what moral attitudes did they have? All their troubles and all their pains and all their struggles had ended in this—a ruined city which time had somehow saved, on this little island in the South Pacific Ocean!

In a way, it was depressing to see this evidence to the uselessness of man's struggles. Man built and man died and what he built lived a little longer—but it was only an etching on the surface of the world. An etching which time would erode, back to the clay and dust from which it had come. The ego of Homo sapiens!

A shiver ran through Dan as he stepped up the pathway toward the huge temple, with its monstrous bird-faced man embracing the city of death.

Each step sparked his imagination and excited Dan's mind. Puzzling questions formed which could never be answered. What kind of people had built and lived here? How long ago had it been? Was it part of a vaster civilization, or just simply what it appeared—the remains of a small primitive city beyond which none of its kind had survived?

Had the people come to an island and built their city—or was it simply part of a larger civilization which had existed on a huge continent in the Pacific, which had sunk, destroying the cities and the peoples that had lived on it? Was this little island all that had remained above the ocean waves?

Finally they came to the temple, whose walls stretched out hundreds of feet on each side of them, reaching dozen feet above their heads. Now red-brown mud, but once beautiful and perhaps covered with gold. The designs left on the remaining parts of the walls were hardly visible.

"Good God!" Carl West exploded in an amazed voice. "What a place this must have been! Just think of the civilization that must have built it. Good God!"

"It leaves the mind frightened!" Billy Turk grumbled, tightening his grip on the rifle in his. "Leaves you feelin' that eyes are watchin'! That the dead are keepin' a silent watch!"

Dan ran his eyes along the huge walls, amazed that so much was still standing. Age was etched on every visible surface. There were portions where the wall had crumbled to the ground, leaving huge gaps in the structure.

They were standing at the entrance to the temple, which stood twenty feet high and at least that many feet across. The doors had disappeared with time. Beyond the entrance was mostly darkness, broken only by spots of sunlight, which revealed nothing but silent emptiness.

For a long time the four stood there, before the huge stone steps leading to the entrance, not speaking, only silently observing.

Dan finally cleared his throat and said: "No reason to stay here all day—just be careful and do touch nothing...be careful of traps.

"How anything could have survived so long, I couldn't imagine. But your Uncle Frank found several—and I think some of his men were killed by such booby traps—so be careful!"

Dan lifted his rifle, pointing it before him, as if to give better protection from ghosts of the dead city—ghosts which could never feel the pain of a bullet ripping through dead flesh. But it gave Dan a sense of security that he realized was false. Yet he needed it.

Moving slowly forward, Dan started up the steps and then finally stood level with the entrance. For a moment he paused, as if afraid of taking that last step across the threshold. Once he had entered the temple, what horrors would they find?

There was a sense of impending danger ripping through his guts. His heart was throbbing painfully inside his chest, and he could feel the sweat begin to pour from his body. Shaking his head, Dan moved forward, past the entrance, and then turned to face the others.

They were standing there just staring at him, as if he were some kind of horrible monster. "Come on—there's nothing in here except us ghosts!"

Ruby laughed and moved to his side. "There's something about the place that gives you the creeps!"

"Just because it is old and—strange!" Dan told her, smiling.

Billy Turk moved to their side. "This ain't nothin' like a lively village!"

"It isn't Grand Central Station—if that's what you mean, Billy!"

Carl West stood staring at them for a short time, and then he laughed nervously and moved into the temple with them. "Well, let's get going!"

Dan felt annoyed, and wanted to slap the younger man around a little. The open horror in the guy's face showed fear. Yet he acted.

"This is silly!" Dan exploded angrily. "We're acting like a bunch of children. This place is an old dead city—that's all. We're treasure hunters—that's all. We came for a little money...so what's this crap all about?"

"Take it easy, Dan," Ruby told him in a gentle voice.

Dan nodded and turned his eyes to Carl. "You

90

know the way to The Virgin Venus?"

"The manuscript by heart!" Carl boasted

"Then lead on," Dan directed, motioning him to the front.

Carl hesitated, his eyes flashing nervously around him, taking in the darkness of the temple, and then he sighed. "Anybody have a flashlight?"

Billy pulled one out of his pants pocket and handed it to Carl. "Here ya are, matie!"

Carl nervously turned it on, and flashed its strong beam around the room where they now found themselves.

All the walls were weathered and crumbling, but there were parts still intact, where they could see the engravings that some long-dead artist had created. At several places some color remained. Most of the paintings were of people working in fields, with hooded men over-seeing them. The eyes of the overseers were slanted and Oriental looking, while the workers were more Caucasian in appearance.

A chill inched its way down Dan's back, and he found himself gripping the rifle tighter until his fingers hurt from the pressure.

"Will ya take a look at that, maties!" Billy Turk exclaimed breathlessly.

"One thing it shows," Ruby pointed out in an even, businesslike voice, "that the city was ruled by temple priests, and the slaves were at least white. There's an—"

"Cut it out, Ruby!" Carl snapped. "We aren't interested in a lecture right now!"

Dan wanted to tell the man to go to hell, but decided to let it ride for the time being. "Let's get going!"

Carl stood thinking for a moment, and then said:

"It must be this way—" Taking a step to the right, he motioned the others to follow.

For several minutes they crossed several darkened rooms, moving carefully from door to door, being sure not to touch anything but the floor beneath their feet. Then suddenly they found themselves moving down a corridor that twisted to the right. Turning, they discovered a huge room whose ceiling had fallen away onto the floor. The side-wall to their right was crumbled to the ground, but at the opposite end of the room was an entranceway leading downwards.

"That should be it!" Carl announced, stepping boldly forward. "That should lead to The Virgin Venus!"

The others followed, excitedly. The gloom of the darkened outer rooms had lifted as they finally arrived at their final destination. Excitement lifted their spirits as they stepped through the entrance and started downward into the blackness, where no sunlight had ever been.

They circled downwards along the narrow stairway, circling around and around. Then finally the beam of the flashlight showed the bottom of the stairway.

Carl flashed the light out in front of him, into the darkness beyond.

They suddenly froze, startled and overwhelmed at the sight before their eyes.

* * * * * * *

The march through the jungle was an agony of

insects and bites to Anna Torrie. She thought it would never end. The passage was already cut for them, and it was just a matter of following the path the first group had taken.

Derk and Jake were in front and Jim Gordon behind her. They had been traveling for a little over twenty minutes when they came to the swamp.

"Oh, God!" Anna screamed in disgust. "I can't go through that!"

"Shut up!" Gordon snapped, pushing her forward. "You could have stayed on board—but you had to go with us! You gotta talk big! Get your big rump moving!"

Gordon shoved her again, and for a moment Anna had to fight back the urge to turn and slap his face. Or ram his balls with her knee. But not yet. There would come a time when she would lose control and he'd get his payback.

"Which way?" Derk asked, not moving, merely standing before the swampy area, staring. Obvious he didn't like the idea-of going through it.

"Straight. They gotta have gone that way!" Gordon announced.

Anna felt a stab of anger mount in her. Gordon didn't have any reason to believe they were headed in the right direction. He couldn't know for sure, because there wasn't any marked pathway in the swamp area.

As they pushed forward, the water rose up around their ankles and then to their knees. Then bit by bit it started to fall away.

Finally the swamp faded out, and they found themselves in a thick jungle. They quickly pushed through the thick underbrush until they reached a rocky area that worked up a hill.

"Can't be much further!" Gordon told the others. "The guy that told me about this place didn't know nothin' about how to get here—but he said it was after the rocky grade—this must be it!"

"Let's get after them!" Derk exploded, starting to move forward.

"I can't go much further!" Anna cried out. Her feet were in agony and her legs aching "Can't we rest for a while?"

"Stay here, if you want!" Gordon snarled, starting to step past her.

"No—I'll go with you...!"

Anna started after him, trying to catch up. Finally they made their way up onto the level ground and stood staring across the ruined city.

"Ain't that some sight!" Gordon exclaimed. Taking out a pair of field glasses, he scanned the ruins. He studied the huge building rising before a backdrop of rugged cliffs.

"There they are!" he exploded, focusing the lens. He watched for a while and then turned and looked at the others around him. "They just went inside—that big building in back! Come on—let's go after them. *Hurry!*"

They started off through the city, unaware of the one-time splendor of what had been there.

CHAPTER THIRTEEN

Dan Shon felt that shiver chilling his spine again. It seemed as if it was one continued chill after another, since he'd set foot on the island. He couldn't help the feeling of being in a graveyard. Now, staring at the huge statue in the center of the large room, he found it hard to even take a breath. It seemed as if everybody had stopped breathing. Then suddenly there was a sharp intake of breath. "The jewels! Where are they?" screamed Carl West in a frantically excited voice. Dan suddenly took in the details of the golden statue centered in the room on a high platform. The arms of the young girl were stretched above her head, and in one of them was a slender knife, pointing downward, as if she were about to strike somebody dead.

The innocent expression on her features looked down at them, blank and yet all-knowing. All over her face and body there were tiny holes, where once must have been a fortune in jewels.

A murmur sounded, and each started forward, circling the statue. Dan was the first to speak. "Where the hell are they?"

"Somebody took them!" Carl cried out. "Some rotten bastard took them!"

Ruby laughed shrilly and then said: "Looks like

the whole thing was a waste of time. Maybe Uncle Frank was right about this place! It wasn't for us— or for anybody!"

"Somebody took them!" Carl yelled again, his face distorting into ugly anger. "Who? Who?"

Dan looked down at the floor, and suddenly saw what looked like footprints in the thicker dust of the ages. The footprints were dusty, too, but not as thickly covered as the rest of the floor.

"Hey—flash that thing over there!" Dan shouted, pointing. "Maybe we'll find our answer!"

Carl moved the flashlight where Dan had indicated, and the others quickly gathered around.

"That doesn't mean anything!" Carl snapped.

"It could have been the steps of your uncle's people—and then it could have been someone else! We don't know!"

It took several seconds to find any new footprints that could possibly be made out of the shuffling of the many scattered around the dust of the floor.

A neat, even set walked right straight toward one wall and then stopped.

Dan quickly started tapping the walls with the butt of his rifle, and after several seconds he felt part of it give. A section of stone moved slightly. Quickly he pushed harder against the slab with the rifle, and it moved several inches.

"Look, matie!" Billy Turk shouted in surprise.

The wall in front of the footprints, where they seemed to step into it, suddenly started sliding away.

Dan pushed again at the slab, and the wall opened more, until there was an opening big enough for a man to step through.

"Come on!" Carl exclaimed, flashing the light beyond the opening.

Billy Turk was first to go into the chamber beyond the wall. The others heard him curse out loud and then shout.

"There's somethin' in here!" he cried. "Bring in the flash!"

Dan moved Carl in with him. Then, as the flashlight moved to Billy's feet, he gasped out a startled breath. Lying there were the browned remains of a human being. What was left of the skin was stretched across the bones like dried leather.

"Stay out there, Ruby!" Dan called back over his shoulder. But his warning came too late.

For a moment Ruby froze, and then a scream choked in her throat. She turned and buried her head on Dan's chest. He ran his arms around her shoulders and told her to take it easy.

"What's this, matie?" exclaimed Billy, suddenly.

"Looks like a book!"

Dan looked over at the other two. They had the light on the corner of the room. There was a table and a little book. "Don't touch it!" he ordered them.

"Why?" Carl demanded.

Dan released Ruby and stepped over to the corner of the small cell. He looked down at the book; then carefully he reached out a hand and gently started to open the book.

It opened automatically to one of the middle pages. The first pages were stuck together by time.

On the page were neatly written words and some dates.

"Flash the light closer!" Dan told Carl. As the light covered the page, Dan started reading:

> **MAY 2, 1931.** Frank has gotten the fever. He is raving about his lost fortune and about the jewels of The Virgin Venus. I'm doing what I can for him.

> **MAY 3, 1931.** Frank is getting better today. The worst is over, I believe. But still I've hidden most of the jewels. Just in case he tries to kill me for them again.

Dan turned and looked up at Carl. "What do you make out of it?"

"Don't know!" the younger man answered, his face concerned and puzzled.

"To continue..." Dan said, starting to scan the page. He carefully turned the pages and then an entry caught his eye:

> **MAY 15, 1931.** Frank West said he was going to leave with his part of the take. That he had to return before—

It broke off there, suddenly, at the end of the page.

Dan turned to the next page. It was blank. Then the next. Quickly scribbled in shaking handwriting was the last entry:

> West has left me here—to die. But he

didn't get the rest of the jewels. I think the fever has made him quite mad. The wound is turning—I know I'll die here—with the treasure that I fought to keep...If only...I'll die here in this room where I buried the treasure. Poor, poor Frank.

It was unsigned.

"In this room!" Carl West cried, his voice trembling with excitement. "In this room!"

"Shut up!" Ruby whispered.

"What?" Carl demanded, turning his eyes savagely toward his sister.

"Quiet!" Ruby cautioned. "There's somebody out there!"

A sudden quiet broke over the small room. The flashlight went dead and they were in darkness.

Dan listened carefully. For a long time he didn't hear anything. Then came the sound of footsteps and then voices.

"Careful!" somebody said. Dan couldn't make out if it was male or female. He listened, then stepped quietly to the entrance and looked out, standing beside Ruby.

There was a flashlight moving around in the other room, stopping on The Virgin Venus—and then an exclamation of shock.

Dan tapped Ruby and pulled her back from the entrance. He found Billy and Carl in the darkness. Whispering quietly, he instructed them to follow him out, with their guns ready for instant use.

Slowly and quietly leading the way, Dan started for the entrance, and then as they stepped out, moving into the Venus Idol room, he motioned the others to fan out. After they had made a circle of the room, Dan tapped Carl, who was standing beside him.

"Okay—just stand there!" Dan ordered the three figures who were examining the statue. "Don't move!"

"What the hell!" one of the men shouted in surprise.

"Freeze! There are several guns on you!"

The three men didn't move. They were as still as the statue.

"Okay—now! Drop your guns—carefully!" Carl had flashed the light on the three men, and Dan watched as they dropped their guns, which clattered to the floor. "Okay—you might as well tell us who you are! Turn around slowly!"

As they turned, Carl exploded with: *Gordon!"* Then he added: "That's the bastard we were running away from...how'd he get here?"

"We followed you," Gordon said nastily. "What do you plan on doing to us?"

Dan spoke. "I don't know. That all depends."

"Kill them," Carl demanded. "That's what they'd do to us!"

"What'd you follow us for?" Dan asked.

"What do you think?" Gordon snapped. "For the jewels you stole from this statue. But I don't know how you got them out so fast!"

"We didn't! Somebody was here before us." Carl asked: "How'd you know how to get here?"
"Knew the guy that was here with Frank West years ago...He knew about the island—but that's all. I wasn't sure that he wasn't just raving—until I found

out about you and...it was easy to put two and two together."

"Then you planned the whole thing...the gambling debt and everything!" Carl accused, angrily.

"You bless your stupid hide! You were a first-rate sucker!" Gordon laughed.

"But the laugh's on you!" Carl snarled, pointing his gun at Gordon. "Now I'll just take care of you, but..."

A shot exploded in the chamber.

For a sudden moment Dan thought Carl had killed Gordon, and then as the younger man slumped to the floor, the flashlight clattering and then going out, he knew that somebody had shot from the darkness.

Who?

Another shot sounded, and he saw the direction of the flame. From the stairway which led up to the surface.

There wasn't time to think or reason things. Action was all that was left.

Dan flattened himself, firing at the entrance.

There was the shuffling of feet and bodies, and he heard a curse from where Gordon and the other two men had been. Then the sound of a bullet, spurting from a gun from their direction.

Dan felt stone chip next to his feet, and he shifted his position, sliding quietly back.

The chamber was in complete darkness, and suddenly there wasn't a sound. The silence of a tomb had settled over the room. Nobody was moving.

Dan hoped Ruby and Billy didn't change their locations. If they did, there wouldn't be any way of telling friend from enemy.

Slowly the silence became loud with breathing. Breathing from several directions. Breathing that was heavy with tension.

Carefully Dan took out a pack of cigarettes from his pocket, making sure he didn't make a sound. Then he threw the pack a couple of feet from him.

There was a light sound as they hit the floor. A gun flashed in the darkness. A bullet smashed into the general location of the cigarettes. In the flash of the bullet, Dan could make out the features of one of the men. He fired and at the same time rolled on his side.

There was a moan and then a curse of pain.

Then silence.

The dark, quiet battle had begun; a battle of tension in the death chamber of *The Virgin Venus!*

CHAPTER FOURTEEN

Dan lay in the darkness, listening to the breathing and not sure whether it was his friends or the enemy. Darkness and black silence. Waiting.

A shot spurted in the darkness.

Dan returned it, twisting to one side as another bullet smashed into the floor where he had been lying.

Silence.

There was a shuffling and then a noise to the right, followed by a blast of fire. It was returned from two sources.

Silence.

Blackness dominated the dead chamber.

Dan could hear his breath hissing in his ear and his heart bursting in his chest. Wetness was dripping from his armpits. A bead of perspiration formed on his eyebrow and dropped over his eyelid.

He didn't dare move.

It seemed hours. Bursts of flame ticked off the minutes. One down. But he didn't know which side had been hit. The blackness was so thick, it was impossible to see an inch beyond his eyes. Nobody seemed to move except to fire, and then their positions changed as the bullets echoed through the room.

Lying there, Dan wondered if it had all been worth it. Thinking back, it all seemed incredible. First, meeting Ruby West, and then her request to take her to an island to pick up her brother.

Then the story about this island and the lost city and the treasure that was supposed to be there. Now this—facing death in the darkness, against people he had never known existed before this afternoon. Each side blindly trying to kill off the other. At least two men dead or seriously wounded.

Was it worth this?

Was it worth it? And Ruby and her seductive body; her hypnotic power over his passions. Her flaming body and her luscious bed charms. All because of a woman.

Curse women! He angrily thought, tightening his fingers on the gun.

Dan's finger squeezed the trigger, aiming his weapon at the dark noise to his left, which had sounded for but a split second.

He heard a cry of pain and then a moan.

Dan twisted to his left, moving just in time as a bullet smashed into where he had been before. He fired again, wild this time.

He rolled over.

Silence.

Just the live breathing of people around him. But this time there was one less person breathing. His only hope was that it wasn't Ruby or Billy that he had hit.

A shot came from his left, just a few feet away. He twisted and was about to fire when he saw the features of Billy Turk, lighted as his shot was returned from across the room.

Dan reached out and tapped Billy gently. For a moment he thought the other man was going to attempt to kill him, then he felt the arm relax. Billy fired at the far wall, then rolled over toward Dan. Their heads almost bumped in the darkness. Dan placed his mouth next to Billy's ear. "Gotta circle together. Where's Ruby?"

Billy didn't say anything. Instead he just nodded and tapped Dan on the shoulder, to let him know that he understood the instructions.

Slowly they edged their way—trying not to make any noise. Dan's gun scraped something in front of him, and the sound sent off three shots from all around them.

The Venus Idol! He'd touched the Venus Idol!

Dan took cover and then reached out for where Billy had been. He found a limp body.

A sickness welled in his gut, and for a moment he thought he might vomit. Finally he gained control of himself.

If he had the *Venus Idol* between himself and the two remaining enemies—if Ruby was the one behind him—then he could take a chance. He'd be protected by the *Venus Idol* from the other's fire—and he could let Ruby know where he was.

"Ruby!" he shouted, pointing his gun in the direction in which he believed she was, at the same time sidestepping.

A rifle spurted flame. Dan returned the fire and was rewarded by the sound of a body falling to the floor.

Silence followed. If Ruby was alive and on the other side of the statue, then she knew the location of the last of the newcomers. If she was already dead—Dan felt nausea flood through him. Ruby couldn't be dead! He didn't care about the treasure or anything. About nothing but Ruby! Suddenly Dan realized that he was in love with her.

Ruby couldn't be dead! He needed her more than anything in the world.

And just as suddenly, he realized the chances of getting her were probably zero. She had given him her body, only to get him to take her here. It was a pure business deal and nothing else.

Suddenly there was the sound of movement and then running feet. They were headed for the stairs. A gun fired, flashing in the darkness.

Another shot sounded, as Dan rushed around the statue and fired in the general direction of the running footsteps. One thing he knew was that it could not be Ruby, because if she were alive, she was pretty sure that he lived and wouldn't be running. The footsteps continued, fading.

Dan waited a moment and then softly called out, "Ruby!"

There was a moment's pause and then he heard her answer. "Over here! The last one went up the steps—he won't be bothering us any more!"

"I wouldn't plan on that," Dan said. "Anybody else alive?"

No answer in the darkness.

"Carl—Carl..." Ruby choked out in desperation. "He's dead...Billy?"

"Dead!"

Dan moved in the direction of Ruby's voice, and then, groping, finally found her. She folded up in his arms, her body trembling.

"It was...awful!" she sobbed.

106

Dan found himself wanting to comfort her. He slid his arms around her body and pulled her close to him. And overwhelming wave of tenderness flooded over him. All he wanted to do was protect her, hold her close; be with her.

The silken, giving quality of her body seemed to fire heated desire. It was the wrong place and the wrong time, but he wanted to kiss her and make love to her. He wanted to always make love to her.

She softly shivered against him, sobbing. It was a long time before her body seemed to stop trembling.

"Oh, God, poor Carl."

Dan didn't know what to say, so he simply held her close. Her breathing became less rapid, more calmed.

"I'm sorry. Not the time...for grief!"

But she still wasn't ready to be released. She clung to him like a little child, desperately wanting, needing comfort.

It was a long time before they parted.

Slowly they stood and Ruby said: "There's a light somewhere on the floor—or with one of the dead..." Her voice faded out as if she were unable to say the rest. "Oh, God! I never killed a person before"

"Maybe you didn't," Dan told her, gently. "Here, help me find a flash."

"Let s get out of here!" Ruby pleaded. "I can't stand it down here any more. Just let me out— please—out of here!" Her voice had the edge of hysteria to it.

Dan reached for Ruby and led her toward the steps. Slowly they felt their way up each step. They had gone up about twenty steps when a rifle poked into Dan s stomach

"Just stay!" said a rasping voice. A rough female voice. "Freeze."

A light flashed in their faces. Dan was momentarily blinded

"Drop your guns and then turn around. We have something down there that I want. Something you came to get!"

There was a pause and then the voice added, "Okay, turn around! Hurry! I don't have forever. I don't like this place. I want to get it over. Turn around!"

Dan and Ruby dropped their guns and did as ordered, returning to the chamber of *The Virgin Venus*.

CHAPTER FIFTEEN

When they reached the chamber of the Venus Idol, the woman stopped them and asked, "Where'd you put the jewels?"

Dan sighed and then said, "You probably won't believe me, but we never saw them!"

"You're darn right I don't believe you! And you'd better come up with them, or I'll be putting a bullet in your gut! First the lady and then you!"

Then she added: "And if you don't think Anna Torrie will do it—just let me point out that I was the first to fire a gun!"

Ruby gasped, "You bitch! You—you killed Carl!"

Ruby took a step toward the voice behind the flashlight.

"Don't do it, dear, or you'll get yours right now!"

"What makes us think you'll let us live?" Dan asked, "if we do tell you where to find the jewels?"

"Take my word for it that you'll live longer that way. There's only one boat and I don't know how to work it."

"One boat?" Dan asked, puzzled.

"Jim Gordon had yours burned! Now he's gone, just like he should be."

The voice took on a softer sound.

"All I want is what's coming to me. I've put up with men like Gordon all my life—and it hasn't been good. So with my cut of the jewels I'll be set for life. That's all I want. To be free of slobs like Gordon!"

Ruby exclaimed: *"Cut?"*

"Sure—you two can take a fourth. You get to live only if you take me to the first port we can find—we'll not worry about the rest of these slobs. Leave them here. Dead where they belong."

"Okay—we'll show you where to find the jewels!" Dan told her. Turning, he led the way to the small room beyond the wall. Once inside, he moved to the stand with the book left by the long-dead, nameless man as a record of his last adventures.

"This will tell you the truth of what I said about us not having the jewels. They're somewhere in this room...but we don't know where!" Dan told her.

He pointed to the book, stepping a little closer to the woman, at the same time shifting his weight so that he was ready for instant action.

The woman did what he had expected her to do. Instinct caused her to drop the flashlight toward the place he had pointed. At that instant Dan leaped.

Darkness followed when Anna Torrie made the mistake of lowering her flashlight. At that point Dan yanked the gun from her hands and pushed her back against the wall. In the meantime Ruby had found the flashlight in the darkness and turned it on.

Dan looked into the features of an attractive woman in her late thirties. She must have been quite beautiful years before, because the lines of age had only given her a sadness around the eyes and a maturity about her features. There was a frightened look on her face.

"Relax, Miss Torrie! I'm not going to kill you. We need you as a first-class witness."

Ruby asked: "For what?"

"We take her back to the authorities, and tell them about what happened here. She'll either sign a confession and statement about the whole affair before we leave the island, or we leave her here in this room to die!"

Terror clouded and distorted Anna Torrie's face.

"You can't do that!" she choked out in desperation.

"Then you'll do as I request?" he demanded coldly.

After a moment the woman nodded, closing her eyes.

"So close! So damned close!" she moaned.

Ruby suddenly burst out with a cry of alarm. "What the hell are you talking about?"

"What do you mean?" Dan asked, surprised by her reaction.

"About the jewels. You aren't going to leave them here, are you?" she gasped.

"Why not? We have several dead bodies here to account for—we can't just leave them here and forget it all. And anyway there are too many complications...these people can't just disappear into thin air.

"The only way we can get anything out of this is to turn it over to the authorities. We'll be getting a clean cut. Enough money to make it worth our efforts."

Ruby didn't say anything for a long time, and it seemed to Dan that she would never make a reply.

Finally she sighed and then said, "I guess you're right. And I don't think I really care about the treasure anymore. It's cost too much!"

She paused and then added in a sad voice: "Poor Uncle Frank—no wonder he had left this place a secret! He'd planned to come back here all along—I guess. I remember something about the stock market crash having broken his money and business. I never did know how he had rebuilt it.

"I guess we know now. This poor fool lying here died...Carl—and Billy...and those others out there. Maybe the cost was too great, I don't really know."

Ruby sighed tiredly again. "Let's get out of here!" Dan motioned Anna Torrie to move in front of him, and they followed her out of the room, across the chamber of *The Virgin Venus* and then up the steps. Ten minutes later they were breathing the fresh air of the outside world. It seemed as if they had stepped out from the dead into the living.

Even the ruins around them didn't have the mystical horror they had first held.

"What are we going to do about the bodies?" Ruby asked in a weak, shaking voice.

"We'll have to bury them before we leave. There's nothing else we can do," Dan told her.

The next hours were a nightmare to Dan. They went down into the black darkness of *The Venus Idol* chamber, with only the light of the flash to break the blackness surrounding him on every turn.

It was ominous work burying the dead bodies of those who had fallen in the battle. He could almost feel the ancient dead of the city, who seemed to be lurking at every curve and corner and inch of this gloomy place. In those hours of lifting the heavy forms of the dead, Dan had a lot of time to think. A lot of time to face himself and his life.

They had come to Tellbrooke Island for the purpose of gaining a fortune. They had come to rob the City of Death, of the treasures it had held in its vaults for centuries, placed there by long-dead hands. Treasures of a civilization, which must have died long before the dawn of modern man. It had possibly existed before the Roman Empire had even been a dream of, even before Alexander the Great had conquered his world. And all that had taken place in the history of Western Man had passed after this ruined city had been built—and maybe even after it had been left to die by itself.

What had happened to all those souls that had lived and died here? Where had they gone? Disappeared into the dust. And was it true that this was the last outpost of a civilization which some called Mu? A continent which spanned the Pacific Ocean, and which had fallen into the sea, to leave only this one reminder of what may have been the birthplace of all humanity.

Maybe they would never know. Maybe scientists would come and explore the city, and find it to be merely the remains of a small race of people who had advanced far enough to build a large city, but never advanced enough to touch the outside world, beyond their island.

As Dan returned for the last time, to take up Carl West, he found himself moving into the small room in which they had found the skeleton of the dead explorer who had returned to the island with Frank West.

Somewhere in this room was a treasure that could make him rich for the rest of his life. Somewhere, hidden, was a fortune that would set him up so that he wouldn't have to work another day—so that he could settle down and live a happy life.

The thought made him pause, standing in the middle of the room, thinking.

But what was there for him? What was left? Maybe Ruby? He didn't really know for sure. Right now, she needed him to return her to civilization. But what would she do then? And what was more important—did he really want her? Was he in love, or just fascinated? And then, did it really matter? If he could find the jewels—then—then he would have all he needed to get all the women he desired.

Dan took the .38 from his pocket and started tapping the walls of the room. He circled three times, tapping and listening for any sound of hollowness.

Sweat was dripping down his face and he felt as if his whole body had been dipped into water. Again he went around the room, tapping each stone in turn. Nothing.

Sighing, Dan went down to his hands and knees and then started on the floor. He was just about to give up, when unexpectedly there seemed to be a difference of sound between the new stone he tapped and the ones he had been tapping.

Trying again, he heard the difference. Suddenly his heart was pounding faster, and all he was aware of was the excitement of somehow removing the stone from its place on the floor.

For several seconds he felt around the edge of the large stone, which was a little over two feet square. Then, placing a hand on both sides of it, he discovered that it was loose, as if balanced on something.

It was several fevered moments before he was able to find the center balance, and then he pressed with all his weight. The stone, which was only a few inches in thickness, suddenly flipped upwards.

Dan flashed the light into the hole that was now revealed. For a moment he couldn't believe his eyes; then he reached down, taking up a handful of gleaming, glittering stones.

Stones of all colors. Stones of all shapes. Diamonds. Rubies. Emeralds. Sapphires. Everything he had ever heard about. Where had those people gotten them? Where had they come from? What fantastic mines could they have sprung? Maybe he would never know. Maybe it was a mystery which time and history had forever hidden from the mind of man. And maybe it wasn't really important.

A civilization found its ways to treasures. In trading. In mining. In conquest. The fact remained that the people who had built the city had gathered a fortune—and this nameless man, who had died alone and trapped, had placed it here.

Right then Dan wasn't interested in even asking those questions. The only thing he was concerned with was to get a handful in his pockets. One handful would take care of his personal life forever. He wouldn't have to worry about money as long as he lived.

Quickly he gathered up a handful of the largest stones and then replaced the lid on the hiding-place. A sudden bold plan had occurred to him. An idea which would secure this treasure for himself.

Walking back into the Venus Idol Chamber, Dan lifted the body of Carl West on his shoulders and then started up the steps.

The burial was quick and to the point. During it, Ruby sobbed slightly, but said nothing about her brother's death.

Dan had found a shallow place which he had cleared of stones, and placed the bodies in it. Then he had covered them with dirt and more stone until they were completely hidden.

He had a slight sense of inner guilt about an unmarked grave for Billy Turk. A common grave with four little bastards! One of them just a greedy coward. Dan couldn't help feeling sorry for Carl West. He had come a long way to find his destiny and death.

After a few simple remarks over the grave, Dan placed his arm around Ruby and then motioned Anna Torrie to move in front of them.

CHAPTER SIXTEEN

It was getting dark and there wasn't anything they could do but spend the night in the Lost City. Once they were out of sight of the rock grave, Dan turned to Ruby and said: "I'm going to have to tie Anna Torrie...we'll have to stay here."

Ruby simply nodded.

Finding a small ruined building, whose walls on three sides still stood, Dan led Anna inside it and motioned her to lie down.

"I'm sorry about this," he told her, taking off his belt, "But there's nothing else I can think of to do. I can't take any chances!"

The woman didn't say anything, only glaring up at him. Dan strapped Anna's feet with the belt, making it tight, but not too painfully tight. He felt like a bastard, having to tie up a woman, but he knew too well that if given the chance, she would slit their throats.

Tearing off a strip of his pants, he ordered her to roll on her stomach. "I'm afraid this isn't much of a way to treat a woman—but..."

"Go to hell!" she snapped angrily.

Finally he had tied her hands behind her. Standing up, he looked down. "I guess it's not too conformable—but it's better than being dead like Billy or Carl! You'll survive!"

Turning, Dan walked out of the ruined building and went over to where Ruby was sitting, staring blankly into the distance. Stepping up to her, Dan placed an arm gently around Ruby's shoulder.

"Take it easy, kid," he said softly.

For a moment Ruby didn't move and then suddenly she was in his arms, tears streaming down her face, her whole body shaking with frantic sobs.

"It wasn't worth it!" she cried after a little while. Her head was buried in his chest. "It just wasn't worth it!"

Silently, Dan led her down the little pathway that led to a small little building that he had found which was in better condition than the rest.

"You need sleep," he said softly. "It's been a little rough—a little rough!"

There wasn't much more to say; it had all been said in the tragic events of the day.

As they lay down in the small room, Ruby curled up against Dan. She was still crying softly, but didn't say anything. For a long time she lay crying, until finally the sobs became softer and quieter and at last stopped.

Dan didn't move. His eyes were closed, but it was a long time before he was able to rest. He lay there thinking about what had happened, and about the jewels in his pockets.

He hadn't told Ruby yet. There hadn't been a right time for it. Tomorrow would be soon enough. Then he would have other things to say to her.

Finally, sleep settled over his tired body. Exhaustion had at last taken its power over him.

Dan didn't know how long he slept. It was still

dark when movement awakened him. For a long time he lay there, trying to decide what had awakened him. Finally he felt Ruby move.

"You awake?" he asked.

"For a long time," she said softly.

For a moment they were quiet, and then Ruby turned and moved her head above his. "Make love to me," she pleaded in a desperate voice. "Make love to me!"

Suddenly their lips were crushing together, their tongues darting in and out. The sensual taste of her brought his mind abruptly alert and his body fiery alive. Every nerve burned. Every cell in his muscles tensed with the ache of desire. He wanted to make more than just casual love to Ruby. He wanted to be with her for the rest of his life!

The passion of their kisses burst into a flaming demand. Dan found himself stripping the clothing off Ruby, and then removing his own. Then they pulled together, taking in the sensual heat of each other.

Dan ran his hands along the luscious curves of Ruby's body—caressing each hollow, delighting in every swell.

Finally he moved his lips down to the white throb of her throat, and her hand urged him further downward until he was caressing the swell of her breasts with his lips.

She moaned and trembled against him, pressing his face deeper against her, straining up against his hips, sighing and convulsively shaking.

"Now!" she cried between clenched teeth, shifting her body to give him the freedom of it.

And he surged down to her into her, and they

were one. Their bodies thrust furiously at one another without restraint, uncontrolled, hungrily devouring. It continued until the final ounce of strength had burst from them, leaving their bodies exhaustedly clinging frantically together.

* * * * * * *

In the night, Anna Torrie struggled with the bonds around her wrist. For hours she worked desperately. Cutting her hands against the sharp edges of stone, finally she managed to break free. Then it was only a matter of minutes before she had unstrapped the belt from around her legs.

For a moment she lay there, trying to decide what she should do. Her chances of escaping the island by herself were hopeless. She didn't know how to run a boat of any size. But desperation moved her. It was her only chance of survival.

If anybody ever found out the truth of what had taken place on the island, she would be sent to prison for life. If she were lucky, they would give her the death sentence. Life had been hard enough, but the idea of dying was even harder.

For a moment she thought of possibly trying to get a gun from Dan Shon, and shooting him in his sleep. But the chances of her doing that were too slim. She had only one chance. Go through the jungle until she came to the boat. There were weapons on it. There, she could kill Dan and Ruby when they came aboard.

Breathing heavily, she came to her feet and started out of the small three-walled room in which Dan had left her. Moments later she was walking out of the dead city, and then starting down the grade.

No thought of the dangers of the jungle occurred to her. It was simply the lesser of two dangers. She had a chance in the jungle—and no chance at all with Dan Shon.

She moved into the night and then into the jungle, and after that across the swamp and into the denser jungle. In moments the undergrowth enveloped her, surrounding her on all sides with the night sounds. The purring of a leopard in a tree above her, as she struggled frantically, almost insanely through the underbrush, didn't attract her attention. She moved.

Then suddenly a clawing, snarling body smashed into her back. Terrible, savage claws clamped onto her throat and in that last moment of life, Anna Torrie screamed out one last desperate cry into the dead ears of the world:

"All for nothing—!"

EPILOGUE

Dan Shon woke up with a dry taste in his mouth. He felt the need of a drink, and reached over to the bedstand next to him. For a moment he thought he was still in the city of the dead. But he was getting used to that. For weeks now he had been having nightmares. He knew that with time they would go away.

Then he turned to look at the woman in bed with him, Ruby was as beautiful as she had been when he had first seen her. Not even those hectic days had left a mark on her.

"Hey—wake up, pretty baby!" he said, shaking the sleep from his eyes. Then he reached out a hand and moved Ruby's shoulder slightly. "Wake up!"

Ruby moved slightly, and turned. She smiled up at him.

"Hello, lover boy!" she cooed, reaching her arms around his neck and then pulling him down to her.

For a long time they kissed, and then finally breaking away, they both sat up in bed.

"You know, Dan, I've never felt so good in all my life!"

"After last night?" he demanded, surprised.

"So we celebrated. So didn't we have reason to

celebrate?" she asked, reaching for the bottle and taking a light drink of the raw rum. For a moment she choked and then laughed. "God! How'd we drink that, last night?"

"What's wrong with it?" Dan wanted to know. "A little too strong for my sober tastes, Danny!" For a moment Dan didn't say anything, and then he said, thoughtfully, "You know—it's a relief to have the whole thing cleared up at last. Now that the island has become government property—I can't say that I feel so badly. We're ahead."

"With that pocketful of jewels, anybody would be ahead!" Ruby laughed, caressing Dan's arm. "And our share of what else they find on the island."

They were thoughtful for a while. Dan was thinking about the shock that hit him when he found that Anna Torrie had escaped. Of how they had gone through the jungle, reaching the boat and then waiting for Anna to show up. They had waited for three days—but no sign of the woman had turned up.

The only conclusion had been that she was in the jungle somewhere, dead. They had finally had to leave. Once they'd reached civilization again, the legal hand of authority had given them a rough time for a while, until things had been checked out.

And finally, almost ten weeks later, yesterday, they had gotten word that everything had been cleared up to the satisfaction of the law. Jim Gordon had been wanted in the States for years. His record supported the statements Dan had made about their adventures on the island. And then, last night had been one series of nightclubs after another. Even on the small island, there were plenty of places to go, and he was sure they had covered every one.

"Dan?"

"Yes, Ruby?"

"What are you thinking?"

"About all that's happened in the past few weeks." For a long time they were silent after that, and then finally Dan turned to Ruby and caressed her forehead. "I've never met a woman like you before," he said in a husky voice.

A throaty sound came from Ruby, and she said, "I have never met a man like you, Dan!"

They kissed lightly, and then Ruby pushed him away. "What's wrong with you? Here it is, probably late in the afternoon—and you want to make love to me! Aren't there other things on your mind besides that?"

"Don't be silly, Ruby!" Dan laughed.

Ruby became serious, and then in a low voice, she said, "It's funny. I lost everything on Tellbrooke—and now I don't feel that I've lost anything of value! Even finding out that Uncle Frank was a murderer doesn't really matter."

For a moment she was silent, and then she continued. "I feel sorry for him—from what the investigators said—he must not have gotten much of the treasure."

"Enough to keep him going for the rest of his life!" Ruby nodded, tight-lipped, and for a moment didn't say anything. Then, sighing, she pulled herself closer to him. "That's all in the past now. We have each other—and that's all that matters! Nothing else counts!"

For a long time they kissed, aware of each other's nude bodies straining together.

There was something about the embrace that was different from the ones Dan had experienced with Ruby before. There was a quality of gentle passion. Tender excitement, loving heat. Not the violent, savage animal heat generated between them before. It was all there—but with different shading. A more wonderful shading.

After a few moments they relaxed. Then Dan whispered in Ruby's ear: "You know—I love you very much!"

Ruby giggled and pressed closer. "You'd better love me!"

They kissed lightly.

"Why?" Dan demanded, pushing away slightly.

Ruby laughed and pulled him closer, firmly against her body. "Why Dan Shon, for an Irishman you sure are a fool!" she exclaimed, pulling his head down to hers.

"What do you think I'm hanging around you for? You aren't getting away from me until you make an honest woman out of me!"

"Then?"

"Then you'll never get away from me!" she said as their lips met once again.

After that they didn't say anything. Instead, they were too busy with the beginning of a lifelong habit: making love to one another.

BOOK TWO

AMAZON GOLD FEVER

And now a look at one of those stories many times published as True Adventures. Here's one that reveals the dangers of having...

AMAZON GOLD FEVER

Maybe I'm not the kind of guy that should complain about a raw deal, but I don't think that really matters. Anybody in my shoes would feel the same way. Raw deal or not, there's a lesson to be learned in my story.

And it is still my living nightmare.

Even in today's world of international terrorist, falling empires and rising new ones, madmen screaming that their fanatical belief systems are the only Truths, the glitter of gold is a blinding light. It is brighter than the mere dark oil that powers modern civilization. Gold has drawn men and civilizations throughout history into its dazzling grip. It is the password to power; it is the universal rock of ages that melts down into riches only the imagination can embrace—it creates empires! Kingdoms rise and fall under its shining glow. And men fall victim to the fever to posses it at all cost.

Well, one has to ask: just how much a price-tag is it worth?

I discovered the limits in a most dramatic, personal, way; a horror story that haunts my life and won't go away.

Few believe my story.

Not that I'm trying to convince people, any more, about the truth of my experience in the Amazon valley. Upriver, into those dark jungles are many unknown puzzles, mysteries and legends. Most are considered fool's stories, or silly myths concerning white natives, golden goddesses, and most of all endless piles of gold. Sometimes it is simply the myths of the ancient Incas, wishful thinking. Sometimes...even the truth is best ignored and passed off as silly fiction. Sometimes the price is too high! Even for gold.

I've tried to convince myself not to tell this to anybody as anything other than fantasy! A nice little story. An adventure. A search for Inca Gold that... But that's the story I must tell now for all to read.

Most readers won't believe this to be anything but a big fat lie, joke, fancy tale to amuse people over a couple of drinks. And not a very satisfying tale, to be truthful. Only that it really happened and changed my life in a frightening way.

Nobody has believed me, so far. And maybe once you've heard my story you won't, either. Hopefully, at least, it'll entertain and give warning to overeager fortune hunters as to the dangers of finding the answer to all their dreams. Maybe my warning will be enough to alert all of you of the dangers that come with a fever for gold.

So, I'm willing to put it down so all can decide for themselves.

Imagine unlimited gold! Well, enough to feed a lifetime ten fold. Trinkets cut into Inca images. Nuggets, just begging to be picked up; gathered together into gunnysacks.

Oh, just the memory of it all, the damned fever pitch that fires the imagination always temps me like some hauntingly beautiful woman offering herself for a life-time of passion.

And the gold fever is hard to avoid when you come face to face with the real thing! And even harder to resist...

We all face raw deals, but when it involves an endless supply of gold treasures just beyond reach...well, to be truthful, that can hurt!

Nobody would like the idea of having a fortune of gold slip through and past their fingers. And the gold is still where I found and left it. The memory of those days will tempt me, taunt me, beg me to go back and get it.

And I never will!

That's why I've taken a little more to the bottle, these past months. Not that I wasn't always a boozer. But rum's a poor way to escape from the memory of that hellish nightmare, yet it is good and cheap—and that's all that counts any more. To put it bluntly, my little adventure into the dimension of Amazon gold fever not only took just about every last dime I had at the time, but also almost took my life as well.

I guess I might as well start from the beginning....

* * * * * * *

I'd been in South America for over two years, bumming from one spot to another. Rio de Janeiro, Porto Alegre, places as far in as Manaus, on the

Amazon River, had passed through my life like a series of drunken escapades. Women had come and gone, and much the money, too.

Finally, about six months ago, I found myself with dwindling funds, enough to last a bit, but the end was in sight—and this I didn't like. The money was part of an inheritance, which my father had left me, and I'd made it quick to all the ports of the world, ending in the beautiful Caribbean—Jamaica, Cuba, Puerto Rico had seen me one time or another—and then finally I gave Brazil a swing. That land of tropical contrasts won me completely and this is where I was now. The three-year fling was nearly at an end, and something had to be done to replace the used up money. That's when I started putting out feelers. You know the method.

"Been thinking I might go into something..."

I'd suggest this to friends. Or just mention something about going inland to the unexplored portions of the Amazon valley. There were still plenty of stories circulating about headhunters with white women goddesses ruling them, of gold fields untouched by civilization. You name the legend and you could buy a piece of paper telling you where such and such fortune could be found. It's all fairy tales, but nice material to dream about. And tempting even for a bloody skeptic like myself.

At first nobody bit. I was left with my face hanging out, a bottle of cheap booze in one hand and a native girl within arm's reach. And some of those ladies can offer up quite a whack-job right through a long night. One can't complain about female companionship in these Latin countries, south of the border, way down beyond Mexico. An

American, no matter how low on big bucks, or in the scale of things, is considered a prime target. And I've never lacked some attraction to the female sex. So this is an ideal place to hide away. Still, even then, it takes money. Even for a bum.

I dropped a lot of hints, let it be known I was to be considered a serious man. Most leads lead to dumb con-deals.

But you can't ask questions too long without getting some real answers. One time, while sitting in a broken-down saloon, slightly under the effects of some tropical liquor which the natives make up and sell for a few American pennies per fifth, I got to talking to the bartender.

He was a pretty chatty guy, and after I mentioned that I was interested in something live to get my financial teeth into, he started telling me about a tribe of semi-white natives several hundred miles inland, away from the River. According to his story, there was a man who had just come from there not more than twelve months ago. At first the whole thing didn't seem to have anything of interest for me. Just another one of those tall tales. Fiction. Or perhaps nothing but a con. Then he mentioned that these primitive folk were almost clothed in virgin gold. That sounded rather fantastic—and down right out of some fantasy adventure magazine.

If I hadn't been slightly loaded I'd have walked out right then—and now I wish I'd done so— thinking it was, at best just another silly legend. But by this time I was not only desperate to find some path to easy money, but also willing to believe any story—no matter how fantastic it might be. Blame it on the booze. Rum can run wild through your veins, make you want to hide inside some woman's arms, or simply pass out in a drunken bliss. Or believe any fantastic tale offered up to stroke your deepest dreams.

"It would seem, *senhor*, that this man Bill Jenson—an American like yourself—was flying over the Amazon when a storm came up out of no-where. His plane finally crash landed and, from his story, just a few miles from this settlement of white natives."

The idea that the guy was American struck me as interesting. At least I could communication in English with the guy, and read him a bit better than when speaking Portuguese. Plus I hadn't seen a countryman for months. That was the real reason for my going and looking the guy up—I didn't even be-lieve the story, really, but the idea of seeing an American struck my fancy. What people will do when outside their homeland to find others like themselves. Instant friendship in a lonely place. People who would never spit at one another are willing to become almost lovers under such condi-tions. In fact, I'd met one rich English woman, a tourist traveling by herself, who was so desperate and lonely that we spend a fabulous week together as long lost lovers. It was quite a raging affair, while it lasted. And don't tell me the English are cold and reserve! She was just about one of the hottest fe-males I'd ever known! And we never even learned one another's last names.

The hotel where this Jenson guy lived was even worse than mine. Once I'd been given his room number and told that he wasn't in I was about to give the whole thing up. The booze was beginning to wear off and my mind starting to think a little more soberly.

"Where's the Cantina?" I asked the clerk, who quickly pointed to a doorway behind him.

The bar was like all other bars all around the world, except that it had only one American in it beside myself. It's strange how a guy gets to recognize people from his own country. The man was American, by the way he sat, by his actions—but not by the color of his skin; it was dark, as dark as a white man's can get from the sun.

If there is one thing that a person can do in a foreign country, it is walk up to a fellow countryman and introduce himself—especially in a place as remote as this. And expect an all-out welcoming. Actually that's how I met that English woman.

"Hello, you must be Jenson!" I said, extending my hand in friendly greetings.

He just turned and looked coldly at me. Never had I seen such deeply penetrating eyes. His expression remained frozen and unchanging. "Who the hell are you?"

"A guy who's going to buy you a drink!" I grinned, sitting down beside him. He just grunted and looked away, staring directly across the counter.

I sat there, studying the man, trying to think of some way to break the chill which he was quite determined to keep walled up between us. Obviously he wasn't the friendly type. Then I decided to simply leap in.

"I heard you had quite an adventure some months back," I bluntly prodded, realizing that the conversation had to move directly to the point, or not at all.

His reaction was explosive shock.

He turned so fast that I was almost knocked off the barstool. Those dark eyes looked at mine for a long time, his lips slowly moving upwards in a tight, contemptuous curl.

"Okay! Who put you up to this one?"

The words came out evenly spaced, as if he were attempting to control some inner, hidden fury.

It didn't take any great intelligence to decide that either he'd been given the needle one time too many or that bartender had yanked my leg at his expense.

I quickly assured him that I was serious and really interested in his story. "This guy told me a little of it, but I had to find out if it was really true. I'll admit I wasn't quite sure—and the idea of meeting an American in this godforsaken place rather appealed to me. Not that many Europeans this deep from the river."

The man calmed some, and then smiled weakly. "Sorry. Just a nasty business…all of it!"

"Want to tell me? I'm all ears."

He laughed at that. "I think there's more to you than just big ears!"

That made me laugh, too, and from then on the relationship warmed enough to make conversation run quite smoothly right in the direction I wanted it to take.

After a couple of drinks came he motioned me into a booth in the corner of the dimly lighted room. Once seated, he told me the following story, in much more detail than outlined here:

The storm had caught his plane,

and when he'd finally been able to manage a landing he had no idea where he was. When he had gotten out of his plane, he found himself surrounded by white savages. Most of them were naked except for a G-string. There were a couple of women in the crowd. Before he had a chance to realize what was happening he was talking to what seemed to be the man in charge. The savage spoke a broken enough Spanish to be understandable.

Then, as his mind cleared from the shock of everything happening so fast, he realized what he was doing and started asking questions. The natives were friendly enough and seemed willing to tell him anything he wanted to know. What he discovered, partly then and partly from his later experience, was that several hundred years before, an expedition of Spanish explorers had gone into the Amazon valley in search of gold and fortune. They discovered it in the valley—but also discovered a tribe of beautiful men and women, suspected of being Incas, or at least distantly related in pre-Columbian times.

To make a long history short, it would seem that trouble developed between the natives and the Spanish and a battle started and ended the whole thing. The Spanish who survived weren't educated enough to even read maps. They stayed on and intermarried.

He was shown some of the "holy" records that the natives worshipped. They turned out to be a Bible and several guns and a map. It was the map which caught his attention. Crudely drawn though it was he could read it easily, and what he saw told him that it gave the directions on how to get to where he was—or how to get back to the river. From then on it would be simple enough to find civilization—but not easy.

They let him make a copy of the map, but wouldn't let him touch it. The night before he left they offered him a gift of friendship. It was a nugget of gold as big as his fist. He had naturally asked where it had been found, but they wouldn't tell him. All they'd say was that it was from the gods. Nothing more could he get from them. When he forced the issue he was ordered out of the village and not allowed anywhere near it, on threat of death. After making several attempts and almost getting himself killed, he gave up the whole idea.

His plane was completely wrecked and there wasn't anything he could do but start out on foot. The journey back to civilization was a long three-month nightmare in which fever struck him hard. When he finally arrived at a plantation he was out of his head. Nobody believed his story. The gold nugget was gone—where, he didn't know. The adventure was finished. And he could get nobody to back a return expedition to get that treasure house of gold just asking to be taken. A few guns would be enough to part the natives of from their Gift from the Gods, if they weren't willing to trade for modern, worthless trinkets.

He had planned on returning with men enough and arms enough to overpower the small tribe, but without money and proof of what he said was true, nobody would back him.

At least that's the way he reconstructed the story. Most of it was conjecture—and as I later learned from actual experience to be fairly correct; it is pretty hard to tell just were myth and truth join hands. There is evidence of some Portuguese culture, but how much is hard to tell. Sure, they speak the Brazilian dialect—broken though it is—yet there could be other explanations for that.

Maybe it was the drinks which made me believe his story. Maybe it was just because I wanted to believe. A desperate man will bite into any tidbit of hope. Maybe only the fact that there wasn't really anything better to do than go along with the ideas which surged wildly in my mind. In any case I decided to believe his sanity—and the truth of the story. I told him that I'd back such an expedition for fifty percent of the take.

Never did a man change so quickly. From drunken, sullen bum to alert, sharp, sure businessman. The agreement was made over a bottle of rum. We wouldn't wait a day. Beginning the very next morning we'd start plans for the expedition and to leave as soon as things could get organized.

It was several days before everything was ready to get moving. We went by barge up the Amazon for the first stage of our journey. This river is a breathtaking sight when first seen from land or air. A curving snake without end, with shining diamond-like ever-changing pinpoints that sparkle in the sun or the dim moon glow.

A watery twisting line cutting through some of the most beautiful tropical jungle and forest lands to be seen on the earth. Eden couldn't have been more beautiful. But a person gets bored and tired of even such glorious sights as hours pull after dragging hours. This first stage was tempered slightly by the small case of booze that both of us had decided was necessary to make the trip up river bearable. Both of us bullshitted about the women we'd known—and both of us kept wishing we had one of them as a playful companion on this trip up the river. Once we even stopped at a small village along the way and found a couple of native girls willing to offer a night in their arms for a few cheap toys and drinks. That helped a little. Beyond that, there seems, in memory, hardly anything to recall about this part of the journey.

We covered a lot of water and miles in the upward trip toward the "end" of the Amazon River. It might be the light drunken haze or my normal lack of direction and distance, but I don't know exactly where it was that we finally put to shore—not even within a hundred miles!

I'd never been this far inland before, and never in the real heart of the jungle. I know some people call it a forest, but to me it's one hell of a jungle! Once we touched land, Jenson never drank another drop of rum. There was a bottle left, which I managed to slowly stretch out for two days. It was a mistake, for this was to be my only chance to discover the real route to our destination.

By the time the dazed fog of liquor slid from my brain we were deep into the jungle and I had no idea of where we were. I was completely dependent on Jenson.

This is when I began to notice the surrounding jungle. Never had I seen so much beauty. Birds and parrots of every brilliant color and combination conceivable—flashing splashes of yellows, blues, greens, reds, oranges, pinks, jet blacks, and purples. And the noise! Everywhere there was noise. If some recording company would come out with a super-power stereo for those sounds...and of course the insects. Though we'd managed to take a nice spray can to cover our exposed skin with its anti-bug chemical magic that actually worked!

It was all charming, at first. Virgin lands, a paradise which lacked only a lovely half naked lady to sooth away the night hours.

Finally even this wore off and the business of walking miles and miles through jungle under-growth became a tiring and torturous thing. Bugs wanted to attack us at every bare part of our skin. The spray usually worked. Spiders seemed to be everywhere, their black, nervous legs wiggling insanely. Then the ants. Harmless ones to biting ones. The jungle lost its glory and became a horrible, slime-infested rot of heat, rain, and creatures of all kinds trying to make a meal out of us. Even the spray seemed to be less than perfect in discouraging some of their assaults on us.

But these little annoyances became a blur, which could be suffered through. It was the other things, which took my attention away from the minor dangers and problems. Snakes. Green boa constrictors! Crocodiles—even though they seldom will attack people, they were a rather frightening, possible danger. Then, once, when starting across a river, one of the bearers saved our lives by dying the most horrible death I'd ever had the chance to witness at the time.

He'd just started across, then suddenly without warning, he gave a horrible scream. This kind of yell is beyond description—for it is the fear, pain, and terror of a man suddenly being eaten alive.

I started to jump to his aid, not knowing what was happening, but Jenson stopped me.

"What the hell!" I cursed at the other man, struggling to be free and help the bearer.

"No! *Piranhas!*" he muttered, gripping tighter at my arm.

I relaxed. The bottom of my stomach began to surge upwards and an acid-like taste flooded my mouth.

Around the struggling bearer was a churning and rippling sea of now-colored water. Red colored water.

The man tried to step backward, but instead fell off balance, into the water. After that it was only minutes before the cannibal fish had stripped his body clean of every shred of flesh.

I doubled over; everything seemed to be turning black, the world fading around me.

I didn't know that this was just the beginning of the gore that I was to witness before civilization thankfully swallowed me up again with its greedy claws.

After that, we were more careful into which rivers and streams we treaded. Jenson seemed to consider the bearer's death as his fault. In fact, it was that incident which was the turning point in our mutual attitudes about the trip. Up to this point everybody had been drunk with gold fever. We had promised the bearers a certain small percentage of the take so that we could get them cheaper and therefore afford more guns and ammunition, but now things were solemn and everybody felt the heavy weight of the dead man's fate. The lighthearted adventuring of the whole affair had suddenly turned into something deadly serious. Nobody smiled. Nobody sang. Everyone took each step forward as if he wished it were two backward.

For the first time I felt like I'd made a mistake. Maybe I shouldn't have started out on this thing in the first place. The idea that I was partly responsible for taking another man's life left me slightly numb and feeling sick. The fact that this man, and all the others, had willingly begged to join our expedition did little to sooth my sense of personal guilt.

We started reaching the highlands, and this was where Jenson became very careful in following the crude line map which he had made from the old Spanish one that some long-dead explorer had created in order to be able to retrace his steps back to civilization. We reached a series of hills and valleys and then finally Jenson explained that we weren't far from our destination.

"Somewhere around here is a river, which we'll follow into the valley where the *people of gold* are!"

True to his claim, we found the river, and a few hours later were in the valley.

By now the fever was upon us once again. The nearness of our destination had brought it back, and every eye and nerve and muscle was alert. The rifles in our hands were ready and the fingers anxious to squeeze the triggers.

The plan was to march into the village and take it by force. From there it would be a simple thing to just move in and make arrangements to have the gold. We didn't plan to steal it, just buy it at robbing prices. Toys of civilization which were cheap to buy but impressive to primitives. Jenson had discovered that the people had needed salt desperately and considered it of great worth, as many primitive people do. With that, we had boxes of other things like colorful plastic beads, lighters, matches, candy, and other minor, cheap things for which simple, uneducated people would give golden rock. We weren't fooled into thinking that they didn't think gold was worth something, but we knew that they wouldn't think it worth as much as a match or a colorful string of beads or any of the other gadgets with which we were supplied.

The next couple of miles were like two thousand. Any moment we expected to be surrounded—and what would happen then we had no way of knowing. But everything went rather smoothly. We passed the wrecked plane which had brought Jenson there the first time. It was rusted red by now. A twisted bird that had died in a crashing death.

The jungle had changed slowly into a light brush land. Trees were scattered all around, with globs of underbrush and vines surrounding them, but they were giving way to the grassland.

We were walking up a rise when Jenson motioned us to be ready for anything.

"Just below this hill..." he whispered, waiting for the others to reach us. Then he ordered silently with his hands that we were to spread out in a long line and move forward.

When we reached the top of the hill everybody came to a shocked and frozen stop. Jenson had known that the village was below us—but he didn't know what we would discover—nobody would be prepared for what was taking place.

There was more activity than seemed possible for such a band of people to cause. From what Jenson had told us about them, he had assumed that there weren't more than around fifty or sixty people in the tribe, but from what we now saw, there must have been two or three hundred.

"Lie down!" Jenson ordered quickly, and the ten of us hurriedly did as he suggested.

The village was several hundred yards away and we were certain that nobody had seen us.

"What do you make of it, Bill?" I asked.

"Can't figure it." He was silent for a moment, then I heard a quick intake of breath. "Notice how they're dressed?"

Just as he spoke I saw what he must be talking about. It was breathtaking. From where we lay it seemed that most of the men were dressed in suits of armor—much like the Spaniards used to wear—but they looked as if they were made of solid gold.

I felt sweat cover my body at the sight. My mind seemed to leap ahead to what might happen if we could get all that wealth into our hands. The world would be ours!

Just then I heard a yell of pain and terror shatter the silence which had surrounded us.

When it comes to action, the human body can react without the mind even being aware of what commands it has given the muscles. I turned and fired without thinking or even really knowing exactly what was happening. All I knew was that we were being attacked. By whom, it didn't matter. Death was seeking us out and there was only one way to escape it. Shoot, and ask questions later.

I shot.

A white savage, covered almost from head to foot with golden trinkets and beads and clothing, fell at my feet, the spear in his hands digging into the ground only inches from my chest—exactly where I'd been lying on my stomach an instant before.

I didn't have time to marvel at the richness in which the attackers were dressed; all I could do was fire bullets at these savage golden warriors. I squeezed the trigger. A man fell dead. There wasn't time to move from where I was lying. All I did was to shift the pistol from point to point.

Five men died under the fire of the gun in my hands. My finger squeezed once more—for the last time. Another man fell.

Then I attempted to leap to my feet. The gun

was empty—but there were still more white savages.

That's when the bottom dropped out from under me as an explosion smashed into the side of my head. Blackness. Spinning. Stars throbbing into existence.

I opened my eyes.

Darkness.

The first reaction was terror. Fear of blindness. I couldn't remember where I was or what had happened last. I started to move, and a hand clamped over my mouth.

"Quiet!"

Then I heard a scream. The scream was something out of a nightmare.

I struggled to be free. Whoever was holding me was stronger was very strong. I was quite helpless.

My eyes became used to the darkness and I realized that it was night and that the sky was overcast with heavy clouds.

Then I saw who was holding me. It was one of the native bearers. When he saw that I recognized him and had stopped my struggling he released his hand from my mouth.

"What's going on?" I whispered.

He explained that the two of us had been left as dead, and that Jenson and the remaining three bearers had been captured and taken off to the village.

"I waited for you to awaken!" he muttered after finishing his brief story. "We go quick! Before it's too late!"

"Jenson and the others!" I said. "What about them?"

"Too late. Nothing that can be done! Dead! Dying!"

I couldn't believe his words. At first I wanted to go to the village and see for myself. Then another scream sounded. It came from the village.

"What is it?" I asked, still too dazed to really think straight. The throbbing at the side of my head was becoming more reality than the world around me. I wanted to pass out and escape the pain.

"Jenson—they torture!"

A numbness invaded my gut. Turning toward the village I took out the binoculars from the case at my side. From this hill I was able to see into the clearing where all the white, golden warriors were yelling and singing and pounding drums. One look at the man who was holding the whole village's interest and attention was all I needed.

I don't ever want to see such a horrible sight again in my life. He had been staked out on the ground, naked, and his stomach carefully slit open—just the outer layer of skin. Most of his bloodied guts were showing. A man stepped up and threw a flaming stick into the throbbing mass of red and gray, the pulsing innards. Another scream, so loud that it almost struck a deafening blow to my ears, sounded from the dying man's mouth. His guts went up in flame, as if they had filled them with some sort of gasoline. It was only a matter of minutes before he'd be dead.

I didn't wait to watch. I didn't wait to even think. Without a word I stood, helping the native bearer to his feet—one of his arms was badly cut up, useless.

We turned and half ran from that valley of gold and golden-white warrior savages.

We didn't stop until we hit the Amazon River. How the bearer was able to find his way back seemed a miracle to me. He died a couple of weeks later of jungle fever which had overtaken both of us.

Nobody will believe my story, of course. You can't blame them. They look at me in that knowing way, as if I were trying to pull their legs.

They laugh and say things like: "If that's true, why don't you return? Get all that wonderful gold you talk about!"

I try to tell them I have no way of knowing where it all is. I wasn't very smart about the journey in and certainly not in any condition to understand our desperate route back to the Big River. It is all a terrible blue. Even then, though, the sight of that burning man is always a killer of any fevered wish to return. It would take an army to overpower those savages. Even if you could find them and get in close without being discovered.

That was a mistake we'd made; being overly confident and believing they were nothing but a few primitive villagers. Apparently what he'd seen that first trip was only a small representative of what was, no doubt, a larger community of people hidden away in the depths of the jungle. A lost tribe, which had survived, all these years, generations, without anybody finding them until my friend made his accidental discovery. Primitive but not stupid.

We blundered. Yet would it have mattered what we did?

Still that doesn't matter, because I couldn't force myself to return to that place, even if I knew how to find it again.

But it has taught me one thing: there is more

truth to some of those fantasies which tell about golden cities, or tribes of white men guarding ancient golden treasures, or of White Goddesses ruling in the depths of the Amazon Valley, than most people will believe. One has to wonder which ones are fantasies and which are actual reports of lost wonders hidden in the depths of the jungles.

Of course most *are* bull.

And only a fool, or madman, would chase after such fanciful tales.

Smart people!

Even the real ones, the true reports, backed by old maps, aren't worth exploring. Not at the price tag. These places haven't been kept secret without good reason—mad though those reasons may be. If there was easy, safe access to such places, they would have been discovered ages ago by other people.

And, of course, the way modern civilization is slowly cutting down the forests it will surely, given time, expose some of these legends as reality based.

Only time will tell.

I know this all really happened to me, one story which nobody will believe—and I wonder about all those others that I'd laughed at before. And how many of them are as horribly real as mine?

Who knows? But someday, when the Amazon has been completely explored and settled by civilization, we'll discover the factual evidence of what lies out there that our legends tell us about with their wild tales that nobody will believe.

But as maddening as it is, even with all that gold out, I wouldn't go back under any circumstances. That screaming man, whose guts were boiling him

150

to death, has plagued my dreams every night since, and will follow me to the grave.

Exploring the Amazon, and seeking golden fortunes, can go to the other mad ones with Gold Fever. The fools who think they can beat the odds.

No fever is worth dying for.

So, here I am, telling my story in print for the first time, knowing that few will believe, and those who do won't take my warning seriously.

At least, now I can put it all to rest, and try to find some sanity in a world gone mad with terrorist, political gamesmanship, international power brokers, you name it, which are even more dangerous threats to life on earth. Maybe our planet won't survive modern civilization. Maybe only small tribes will survive after we've fought our religious wars, after the terrorist has sparked a world wide mutual destruction.

If there's anything to be learned from my little story its that a small group of Spanish explorers were chopped down to a few survivors who intermarried and left behind them this hidden culture which has continued to exist without discovery until recent times. And they now remain lost. That may turn out to be our future—surviving somehow in a new primitive world, groups of people isolated and managing…Empires fall and rise. Rome stopped existing. The English Empire and the USSR simply melted down. China may be the new, future, super power to rise in the twenty-first century. Who knows? But nothing lasts but the myths, legends and the survivors taking on new forms, new cultures, and new histories. Only the natural wonders of the planet continue to last. Even our species may soon go the route of the dinosaurs.

Perhaps the only lesson is that as long as Homo sapiens manage to exist gold will be one of the universal treasures which all cultures will valued as they have throughout history.

We humans are fascinated by its glitter, and have been from the beginning of time. And it will continue as long as there are men to worship its golden promise.

As for me? I'm cured of any gold fever, Amazon or otherwise. I plan on returning to the states, once I get enough cash to buy a ticket. Maybe the publisher will pay enough for this story to get me home.

Until then, well, the nightmares continue; and will never totally disappear.

But...I'll survive.

www.ingramcontent.com/pod-product-compliance
Lightning Source LLC
Chambersburg PA
CBHW031606260626
47154CB00020B/1638